REVOLUTION

A RAW ANTHOLOGY

9th Publishing

Contents

Preface

As I put the finishing touches on this Preface, I find myself basking in the glow of a recent reading I had the honor of participating in. Many days, writing feels like the most solitary act in the world; all of those hours spent alone at the table, drafting, revising, dreaming, revising again, then sending out the work with the small hope somebody will want to help the work find an audience. But after a reading, I am always reminded of the glorious communal side of the writing process. In my opinion, there is no better feeling than sharing a piece of writing with another, and seeing what happens.

An anthology offers us one of those rare opportunities to gather around literature — not in a room, but in a binding — and it's one to celebrate. We are not alone.

In this anthology of Rockford area writers, you'll find poetry, fiction, and nonfiction on a wide range of topics, but what they all have in common is a dedication to the exploration of our beloved city.

It was my pleasure to participate in the genesis of this project, and I hope you enjoy.

Jenna Goldsmith
City of Rockford Poet Laureate (2023-24)

BLOWN OUT AND TUNED UP

BY M.K. DAVIS

It starts with a panic attack
echoing through the concrete structure of your body
Deep shudders crawl under the skin
Wired worms with no place to go
spiraling like ants who've lost the trail
When did the 9-5 become a prison sentence
When did the everyday become a noose
cinching tighter around your throat
clawing for air against the hempen knot of modernity
The Army left your mind as bombed out
bricked out
fallen out
as the country you tried to conquer
The moon dust of Afghanistan still clogs your throat
Yet
here you are
Trying
Attempting
to be something you're not
To be anything but the

broken down

rusted out

beat up station wagon

Still trying to maintain relevance in a world full of

SUVs and

trucks bigger than God

No spouse

No parents

No one to help steer the boat

Your only refuge

a small bookshop in Rockford

Nestled like a cat in a window between

a bar and

a crystal shop

In there you search for an escape

A means to end it

A subtle way to cut the rope around your neck

To uncock the rifle of every bastard

aiming down their scopes

ready to blow your brains against the brick wall

Every post army coworker who called you mentally
unstable

Every boss who called you in to correct your behavior

Uncorrectable behavior

Every person who looks at you like a rabid dog

You go there to escape

It starts with a panic attack

A small revolt against your own body

The prisoners starting a revolution

with sharpened soap made of regret

It ends in a bookstore

It ends in the pages of Frankl

telling you that you can learn from your suffering

That you survived

That you crawled through the wire and made it

to something

to somewhere

Anywhere but oblivion

It ends with Rosner's Café

and the stories of countless others

like you

Not survivors

That implies a passivity on your part

But people who have lived through it

It ends

but nothing ever ends

It only ever begins

The prison riot in your mind turns into something

else

Something

new

A revolution of a different sort

A changing of the mind

Of the way you see yourself

A revolution of thought

carries you away

You're bombed out

You're bricked out

You're blown up

But now you're tuned up

You are more than a shattered vase

The pieces now form a mosaic

A ceramic tapestry of lived experience

You are more than an event

You are fractured

You are whole

ABOUT M.K. DAVIS

M.K. Davis is a writer, father, husband, and veteran who has been warmly adopted by the Rockford arts community. He has just finished his MFA in Creative Writing from Northwestern University and plans on doing something with his degree. Contrary to popular opinion, he is not a wereferret, doomed to shit in corners every full moon.

HEMLOCK HOUSE

BY KIM WALKER

I wasn't always as I am now, so diminished, truncated, pieces of me hacked away by the greedy and the desperate, leaving me so reduced, a shadow of my former self. Once a beauty, near boundless, my myriad emotions played over an ageless face all couldn't help but love. I was clad and painted in the finest of shades, the lushest summer greens and the purest icy whites, oranges and reds fluttering in the crisp breezes, and the palest tones of water skimming my curves and valleys. I was once glorious to behold.

I wasn't always as I am now, so sickly and ailing, pockmarked and cratered, putrid vileness running through my once-pure veins, injected there by the careless and callous. Once, I was bountiful and bright, a shining beacon of health and vitality. I gave and gave, but my cup never emptied, such was the bounty of my spirit. Injury would change me, surely, but never unhealable, never final, always simply a new scar in a vast tapestry of beautiful accidents. I was unbreakable once. *I was.*

I wasn't always as I am now, *hot*, volatile, filled to the brim with limitless rage, wronged again and again by my own creation, for nothing more than convenience and greed. I was once temperate, kind, only giving and taking as needed to make my dear children shine. Grow, flourish, reap, and rest, a predictable cycle of my decisions. Everything reasonable, always rational, even while allowing myself the minor frustrated outburst, as all living beings are allowed. *I was a good mother*. I swear I was.

And now I am this, *this box*, this creation of timber and plaster and piping bursting from my earth like a boil. My four walls stand upright despite me, my shingles layer tightly, housing my fury. My body is a neat quarter acre on a corner, the streets named after a dead President and a massacred nation, in a city named after a river crossing that none even know how to accomplish anymore. I am *this*.

I am older, by far, than my hollow plastic neighbors, who squat soullessly on plots that were once me, my limbs and parts and skin. Their vacant husks cannot begin to imagine the changes I have seen since my eyes first came together in warped panes of bubbly glass. What was my favorite? Electricity, I think, though they had to cut open my walls and stuff me with wires. The gentle glow of early lights soothed me, felt so much like lightning running through me, and, for a time, I hoped that my children would settle, now that they had come full circle back to me. I was wrong. So very wrong. But that is not my story.

Have you seen what lives in the grasslands and forests, in the swamps and the trees and the rushing rivers? Of course you have. You've watched a television. But I had them. I had them all. And I had them *here*. They were mine, my own, my children. I sheltered them in my boughs, in my valleys and crevasses. I fed them with my bounty, my fruits and flowers, my seeds and roots and nectar. And I mourned them, as their home, *my body*, was cut away. I cried as their habitat, *my skin*, was poisoned with sprays and chemicals. I screamed in anguish as they were driven from me, further and further, crushed together in small sections where they couldn't possibly sustain themselves. I grieved as they starved, because I couldn't reach them.

And now I am this. This barren patch of lifeless green. This square of shallow grass surrounded by other squares of shallow, useless grass. I produce nothing. I feed no one. I exist, but sustain none.

Many have come before. I have never stood empty, as these wretched destroyers, once my children, refuse to leave me be. They chop and paint and trim and pull and won't allow me to simply give up, to return to the ground where I began. Each must hack and break the designs of the one before, wasteful and destructive. I rage at them, creaking and cracking, leaking and splintering, but they just patch me up and move on, oblivious to my fury. I hate them. I do.

Then, this one. This one is not as the others. She seems content to let me be. She paints me in shades of what I once was. She doesn't knock down my walls, doesn't break holes into me for vanity's sake. She lets my square of lifeless green grow wild, despite protesting neighbors: weeds sprouting, trees overgrown and tangling, seeds blowing in my breaths of wind. My glass eyes have seen birds alight again, red and blue and yellow and brown. Raccoons, opossums, rabbits, and even coyotes sneak on my tiny patch of wild green, the ancestors of my exiled children. She does not drive them away. She leaves them *treats*. I might not hate her.

I wasn't always as I am now, but perhaps I can be something new. Something devious, something tricksy, a different approach to my previous defiance. For her, I will not creak and crack and sag and splinter. I will stand tall, her paints in shades of my sunsets and loam, sweeping my face like a badge of honor. Instead, a creeping sort of rebellion will seep from my foundations. One even the other squares of green will feel.

First came the pokeweed, and I admit, not my best choice, but their seeds spread so nicely, and I was ambitious. The pale green leaves and trailing white flowers are striking, and the dark purple berries even more so. Birds appeared, delighting in their bounty, while I waited quietly for little grasping hands to stuff them into greedy mouths. Unfortunately, the plant's aggressive nature and height were too much for her, and for the first time, she pulled and tore at me. I snarled and snipped, popping a leak in my roof. More subtlety, then.

The nightshade came next, bittersweet, an innocuous looking vine with delicate leaves. Its dainty violet flowers brought the big fuzzy bees, their bumbling antics adorable to watch. The berries, a bright, shining red, fed the birds, my newly returned friends. She smiled at the pretty tableau, and let the vines be. Best she not eat them though. Not her, anyway.

And now, now we are here. Where we meet, her and I, finally. It started, the hemlock, with just a small spot, the emptiness where a tree was felled. Hemlock, bane of philosophers everywhere, looks like nothing so much as a simple fern with lacy white flowers. To my shock, early in its sprouting, she picked some, and I bit back a creak of protest. Not her! But she showed no ill effects, incorporating my dubious gift into her work. Much to my chagrin, she began to care for the plant, nurture it, coddle this peddler of death on her very doorstep. She wears gloves now. She must know. But we have met in purpose, she and I.

I wasn't always as I am now, but I see now. She has the yearning, same as I. And perhaps others, ones I can no longer see in my diminished state, have the same, this yearning for silent protest, this quiet rebellion.

Maybe I won't poison them all.

ABOUT KIM WALKER

Kim Walker is a writer and copper artist with an unhelpful degree in Photography. When not working on her small business, she can be found reading other people's writing, gaming, and watching too many murder shows. She lives in Belvidere, IL in the real Hemlock House with her husband and 3 aging cats. You can find her and her copper artistry at Linktr.ee/BastAndBaetyl.

WHERE THEY BELONG

BY CAT STARK

B rian felt warmth infuse his body as Bethany giggled. He watched
with love in his eyes as she ran her slender hand through her
blond hair. It was her infectious giggle that made him fall in love with
her in English 101. Tonight, a month after her graduation, and six
months to his, they walked around the Rockford University campus,
hand in hand. His sister Sheila was throwing a party for students still
on campus. They had stopped by to drop off Pickled Sips.

The hard candy and its name were from another realm with a
language not easily pronounceable by humans. 'Pickled Sips' was as
close as most humans could get. The candy was made with honey and
plants not found on Earth. It gave humans a mild high and allowed
them to see magic.

Brian had picked up the Pickled Sips yesterday, from his friend
D'Azal, a mage from a different realm. After taking one each and
dropping off the rest with Sheila, the couple headed out for a walk
around campus. Places where people gathered or felt strong emotions,
like school campuses, deserted malls, historical sites, tourist traps, and
haunted places, were best to see glimmers of magic. For many reasons,
humans seemed to leave a bit of their energy and emotions in those
types of places. That caused pockets of tiny magic to form that could

be seen, if a person knew how to look for them, or if someone used something like Pickled Sips.

Strolling around campus, Brian and Bethany noticed when the Pickled Sips took hold. They could see magic orbs dancing in the air along with fireflies and pixies. The fireflies flashed greenish yellow. The pixies danced about in pastel pink, blue, or green and the orbs' colors shifted and shimmered constantly. The lights filled the air, but gave the couple their space.

Though it wasn't the first time they had taken Pickled Sips, it was the first time taking them on the Summer Solstice. On this magical night, a lot more lights filled the air. Bethany tried to capture one or two, but all were too elusive.

"This is gorgeous. I've never seen so many."

Brian sighed in contentment. "They're here to see the most beautiful woman in existence."

She turned back to Brian, a smile on her lips. "Thank you."

He pulled her into his arms, gave her a kiss, but let go as she moved away to follow more lights. Brian followed her and soon, they found themselves at Adam's Hall Arch. Brian stopped to look at the Arch, as Bethany moved toward its clearing. The large structure was built in 1891 and came from the original Rockford Female Seminary campus. It was right next to Starr Science Center and close to Fisher Memorial Chapel. The walkway was close by, as were the trees. The Arch was an entryway, and still had the concrete, stone, and glass from the original building. It looked and felt old. On the other side of the Arch was a stone bench. A lot of people used it as a make out spot. Some said it was haunted.

"You sure you want to be here?" Brian sounded hesitant.

"I like it. It feels magical."

She reached out to the lights, which floated out of her way, then turned to Brian. Her eyes sparkled with laughter as she slipped her arms around his waist and held him close. She was taller than him by a few inches, which he preferred. Brian smiled as they snuggled close for a minute. When she moved away to look at the lights, he frowned as something scurried in the underbrush.

"There are rumors the Arch is haunted." He said with trepidation; he had never been here inebriated.

She giggled again and searched his green eyes. "We've been here so many times! I've never once heard a noise I couldn't explain."

Brian frowned but didn't move. "I think D'Azal said it's full of magic. Something about it existing in some form or another across multiple realms."

She gave him a look and giggled, as she used the human pronunciation for the mage's name. "I think Dazzle has a crush on you."

He looked away and rubbed the back of his neck as his face grew warm.

"I think you have a crush on them."

He looked back into her eyes in time to see a lot more questions brewing. He narrowed his eyes and looked away quickly. "Beth..."

"It's ok, Brian." She moved closer and placed her hand on his.

"I don't know how you feel about all that." He felt as his voice caught.

She shrugged. "It's not a deal breaker. You've known them longer than you've known me, and you've never done anything about it." She moved away as she sighed. "And I mean, he's a giant cephalopod. Earth cephalopods don't have sex like we do. How would all that work?"

Brian frowned. "I've wondered that, too."

Bethany turned her head to follow the movements of some stray lights as they danced by. She shook her head and giggled. "Wow, this is too serious a conversation for me right now. I don't know why I brought this up. Can we talk more about it tomorrow?

He gave a soft laugh. "Sure."

She looked around the clearing. "This really is perfect, don't you think?"

Brian looked forward and sighed. It was perfect. The trees stirred a bit in the wind. The moon shone through the trees and lit up the Arch in a halo of soft, white light. He frowned, looked around, then nodded. The nearby overhead streetlight was off. As he looked around, worry left him. More and more lights danced about the clearing. It filled him with peace.

"What's that?" Bethany moved forward, towards a steady, flat, purple light.

Before Brian could say anything, she touched the purple light that hovered in the archway. As the shimmer spread, they could hear gunfire and screams of pain. Then, as the portal grew large enough to step through, they saw the other side. Sunlight illuminated a large field of grass, which looked more purple than green. Maybe a mile away, there was a line of trees, with deep green, almost blue leaves.

Something exploded in the other realm, close enough for the couple to feel the vibrations in the ground. They could see dirt flying up where, presumably, a bomb had hit. Brian reached out to Bethany and grasped her hand lightly.

"Back up. We don't know what's going on."

As he started to pull her back, a guttural, gravelly voice full of pain yelled, "MEDIC!"

Brian did a double take. Though the word wasn't in English, he understood it. His eyes grew wide as he tried to pull Bethany to him. Instead of moving back she pulled her hand from his.

"Coming!" Bethany bellowed in English.

Frozen in fear, Brian watched as Bethany leapt through the portal. "Bethany! No!" He screamed as the portal closed behind her.

Six months later

"How goes the search?" D'Azal's smooth voice soothed Brian's raw nerves.

"The Portal Mages stopped the investigation today. Bethany's parents and I tried to convince them to continue, but since she went through of her own volition, they refuse to do anything."

Brian stood at the door to D'Azal's workshop, in the mage's home. He glanced over at his friend, trying not to stare. The six-foot-tall walking cephalopod fascinated him. They walked on four tentacles, and used four as arms. It made them look like they were gliding across the floor when they walked. They had six eyes, situated about the front of their face, more like a jumping spider than an octopus. Brian sighed as he wondered if D'Azal's people kissed, as he had no idea if the mage had a mouth or a beak, like the average octopus. When they spoke, they used telepathy.

All this wasn't what made Brian want to stare at his friend, though. The mage shimmered with magic. Lights danced around the mage, teasing the corner of the eye. It made them look ethereal.

D'Azal's dark blue skin faded slightly, as they agreed with the statement, and brought Brian back to the issue at hand. "That is the rules of portals. If a conscious entity goes through on their own, we're not allowed to pull them back."

"That makes sense if someone knows exactly what they are getting into. But a portal opened in front of her, someone yelled for a medic, and she went through."

"She's a nurse, right?"

"Well sure, but..."

"She did what she felt was right, Brian."

"I still can't..." he shook his head. "It looked and sounded like there was a war going on, D'Azal. Can't you help me?"

The many tentacled mage looked uncomfortable as their skin went dark again. "This is tricky, Brian. The magic will not allow us to pull her back. Even if I was able to find all the elements needed to call a portal, there are too many variables. It may not be possible to find her."

Brian moved closer with a pleading look in his sorrowful green eyes. "Can you try?"

"If we do this, we operate on the assumption that we are going to *askask* her to come home, not force her. It must be her decision."

He nodded enthusiastically. "I can live with that."

D'Azal's skin changed to a lighter blue. "We can try, but you *will-willwill* help me gather ingredients. It may not be easy."

"I'll do whatever I can." His voice was full of confidence.

"Don't say I didn't warn you."

The Summer Solstice

Brian and D'Azal waited in front of Adam's Hall Arch. It was after sunset and clouds hid the moon. The nearby light was broken again, or maybe had never been fixed. Brian felt it was odd, but pushed it out of his mind as the mage worked some spells near the Arch. Their eyes were closed, and four of their tentacles were pointed towards the Arch. D'Azal whispered just under their breath. They warned it would take hours to cast the spell. Brian looked away from his friend as his stomach did somersaults. He told himself it was due to the situation, and not how beautiful the mage looked as the low light glinted off their midnight blue skin.

Brian sighed heavily as the weight of the evening pressed down on his heart. They weren't even here to open the portal to Bethany. They were here to find out if it was even possible. First, they had to find out if the portal was a fluke or a constant. If it was a constant portal that always opened on the Summer Solstice, they then needed to find out if it always went to the same realm or sometimes or never. It was discouraging. There were too many variables, as D'Azal had warned.

After an unknown amount of time, D'Azal lowered their tentacles and opened their eyes. Brian gave his friend a blank stare, which turned hopeful as a tiny purple shimmer appeared in the archway.

"It's an infant portal."

Brian stared at the shimmer. "I don't remember what that means."

"Portals always lead to the same place. Infant portals don't."

"Ok." Despite what his friend said, Brian wanted to touch the shimmer and jump through.

They held out one of their tentacles. "Give me your hand, then touch the infant portal."

Brian nodded, moved forward, and took the offered tentacle. To his surprise, D'Azal's skin was as soft as velvet. He cleared his throat to bring himself back to the moment, then reached out and touched the shimmer. It pulsated for a moment, then stopped.

"Interesting."

Brian looked sharply at D'Azal. "What?"

"This infant portal opens to the realm where the person touching it is needed the most. The fact that it didn't change for you can mean that you are either needed in too many places, needed nowhere, or are in the correct realm."

"That second one is a bit depressing." Brian's eyes shifted left and right. A sigh escaped his lips as D'Azal wound their soft tentacle around his hand.

"You belong here, is what I wish to think."

Brian's breath hitched as D'Azal's smooth skin caressed his hand. The mage's skin felt like velvet against his. Brian closed his eyes as he wondered what it would be like to hold D'Azal close, to feel their velvet skin against his. As his cheeks grew warm, he pulled his hand away, turned, and adjusted himself to relieve the growing pressure in his jeans. He then cleared his throat, turned back to D'Azal, and hoped the mage wouldn't question his actions. "So, what does that mean about talking to Bethany?"

"I must perform another ritual. Please move away."

Brian nodded and moved to the tree line quickly. He turned to watch D'Azal as they continued casting. After only a few minutes, D'Azal turned to look at him.

"I can see where the portal opened to last. It's a far realm, and is currently at war."

Brian looked surprised. "It sounded like a war was going on when it opened last year. I guess I was hoping it would be done by now. Does that make it harder to open the portal?"

"No, just more dangerous."

He nodded in contemplation. "I get that. Are you willing to do it?"

"I need more ingredients. It'll take another year to gather the energy and components for the correct spell. You'll need to cast the spell next year, Brian. Which means I'll need to teach you some things. Are you willing to take that time?"

"Yes." There was no hesitation in his voice.

"Then we should leave. You should go home, get some sleep, and come to my home in the morning. We'll start then."

Brian nodded and tried not to be so happy about spending more time with the mage. "Thank you."

"Please continue to keep this from her parents. I don't want to get their hopes up."

He sighed heavily. "What about *my my_my_* hopes?"

"That is your burden to bear," they slipped one tentacle around the young man's shoulders. "But I can help you carry it."

Brian smiled gratefully, but slumped his shoulders in defeat. He gave his friend a better smile, then the two walked away toward the parking lot.

One Year later

Brian stood before Adam's Hall Arch with a bag of stolen magic in his hands. The leather bag felt heavy, but also weightless. It seemed to shift depending on his thoughts. When he thought of all he and D'Azal had done to get the magic, the bag felt light, as if it wanted to float back to its rightful owners. When he thought of the task at hand, the bag became a heavy burden in his thoughts. Brian did not want to contemplate the reason for that and let his thoughts go.

The young man sighed and stared at the Arch. Two years ago, he came here with Bethany to see magic, and lost her to another realm. He had learned a lot about enchantments in the past two years, but he felt he also learned a lot about himself. He turned his head carefully and caught D'Azal out of the corner of his eye. The mage stood in the tree line, on the other side of the clearing. The time he spent with D'Azal made him happy, but confused him as well. He always thought he would spend his life with Bethany. With her gone, his feelings for D'Azal were harder to ignore.

Brian shook his head and turned back to the task at hand. He only wanted companionship because Bethany wasn't here. Those feelings would pass once she was home, he told himself unconvincingly.

Another sigh escaped his lips, which were turned down in sadness. His mournful green eyes searched the darkness between the Arch and the bench for the flat purple shimmer. It was the right time of night, he just had to be patient. The infant portal had shown itself last year and the year before. D'Azal searched the records and found out the infant portal had shown itself here for many years previous. It would show. There was too much magic for it not to show.

Finally, the shimmer appeared. Brian's eyes grew wide as he started the spell. He opened the bag, placed his hand inside it, and whispered Bethany's name over and over. His hand tingled as his fingers played in the magic. A picture of her came to mind; it was what she looked like the day she left. Her blond hair shone brightly; her brown eyes were filled with kindness. Her mouth turned up in a smile as a giggle bubbled from her thin lips. The mole on the right side of her face looked cute next to her button nose.

Picturing her in his mind made the pain even more real. He missed her terribly. He missed when his pillows smelled of her rose perfume; missed when her work rough hands caressed his skin. His breath hitched as a tear rolled down his cheek. With the image of her in his mind and heart, he moved forward, withdrew his hand from the bag, and touched the shimmer.

"Open to Bethany."

He wanted to say so much more, to demand his love back from the realm that stole her. D'Azal coached him over and over to keep it simple. Magic liked to be tricky. If he said too much such as, "Open to Bethany, show me my love," the magic could open to a realm that held something he loved rather than someone. Brian asked about using her last name, but that was where the image of her came into play. If his mind only saw her, the magic would read that and find her.

As the infant portal opened into a full portal, Brian felt he had the right realm. The field, though rather torn up by war, was the same as he remembered from two years ago. He could still see the odd colored trees on the other side of the field.

"Call her, Brian. Quickly."

Brian nodded, took a deep breath, and called her name. "Bethany."

There was no answer from the other side. There were noises, but nothing that sounded like her voice.

He called louder, "Bethany!"

A large hulking form filled the portal. Brian took a step back as the creature snuffled then moved out of the way, calling, "Anni!"

It looked like a bull walking on two legs. It wore old, dirty clothing, and held what looked like a rifle, but at least it was calling for... someone.

Brian heard that name again and frowned. Before he could call again, someone moved into the portal's opening. His mouth dropped open. "Bethany?"

"Brian?"

Her voice sounded different. The light giggle that permeated her voice two years ago was gone. She sounded older, but still looked amazing. She had always taken care of herself, but now she looked fit, like she worked out. Her blond hair was tied in a bun. Her eyes were bright but not with mirth. He wasn't sure what he saw in her eyes other than surprise. She wore a white shirt and green pants that were splattered with a blue substance.

Brian visited Bethany once when she was working in the ER. She went to lunch without changing her clothes after working on a patient who was in a bad accident. She had been covered in blood and gore. Brian's face went white as he realized that the substance on her clothes, though blue, also looked like gore. He looked quickly back into her eyes.

"Brian, what's going on?"

He stared at her for a moment, then shook his head. "I'm here to take you home."

She looked confused. "What?"

He tried again. "This is your home, Bethany. You belong on Earth. It's been two years since you left. I had to cancel our wedding plans, but we can reserve everything again."

She gave him a look full of wonder and stood speechless for a moment. The look changed, her eyes dropped to the ground, and she muttered something under her breath.

"What was that?" His voice sounded strained, even to his ears.

"Brian, I don't want to leave."

The statement hit him hard. "What...do you mean?"

"These people need me." She was looking in his eyes again.

He could see the sorrow, but wasn't sure why it was there. "But... but we're supposed to get married."

She pursed her lips and looked away again. "Brian..."

He tried a different tactic. "Your parents are worried sick."

She looked around. "Are they here? Did you bring them?"

"No. D'Azal thought it was best if they didn't know we were trying this."

She nodded as if expecting nothing less. "Can you give them something for me?"

Confusion flooded his body. "What? I mean..."

But she had already walked away from the portal.

"Bethany?"

She wasn't gone long. In front of the portal again, she held out a small, folded stack of what looked like red paper. "I wrote these my first few months here. Some are for you; some are for my family. Can you take them?"

Unsure of what to do, other than grab her arm and pull her through, Brian turned to D'Azal. When the mage's skin turned lighter blue, Brian turned back to Bethany. He fought against his thoughts and carefully took the papers.

"Thank you." She sounded relieved.

"You're not coming back?"

"These people need me. They're in the middle of a revolution. They need all the help they can get. They don't have a lot of doctors or nurses. I've been learning and teaching."

Desperate to convince her to come home, words tumbled out of his mouth. "How do you know who the good guys are?"

He flinched at the look in her eyes. It was an old argument. He always thought of war as good versus evil, like in video games. She never thought war was that simple.

"War doesn't always have a good and bad side, Brian."

"I just want you to come home."

She was quiet for a moment. "You could stay here with me?"

His heart sank. "Do they need computer programmers there?"

She shook her head. "No, but I could teach you to be a nurse."

"I can't look at your clothes without getting queasy."

She frowned, looked down at herself, and realized she was covered in blood and gore. "Oh. Right." Bethany sighed and looked back into his eyes. "I'm sorry, Brian."

"The portal is going to close, Brian." D'Azal's smooth voice, usually able to calm him, did nothing to ease his pain.

Bethany looked beyond Brian to D'Azal. "Hello, Dazzle. It's nice to see you again."

The mage bristled at the human pronunciation of their name. It wasn't that they disliked it, it was simply not correct. They moved next to Brian anyway. "It's nice to see you again, Anni."

She glared at the mage.

Brian perked up at the nickname. "The natives are calling you that, aren't they? You hate that."

"It's the closest thing to my name that they can pronounce."

He nodded, then gazed into her eyes. "I don't want to lose you."

"And I'm not leaving here. Besides, D'Azal has a crush on you, and you have a crush on them. You should explore that."

Brian felt his body flush as the portal closed between the two worlds. He turned to D'Azal, his eyes wide. "Um..."

The mage's skin was a rather beautiful shade of light blue. "We could."

"We've been friends for years." He shook his head and looked down at the stack of folded papers in his hand. The letters allowed him to change the conversation. "I can't believe I didn't actually say good-bye."

"You can request to talk to her with the Portal Mages. There will be a fine for what we did tonight, but now that we know the circumstances, we can request permission to talk to her. That way her parents can speak with her as well."

Brian glared at his long-time friend. "I have a feeling you knew this would be the outcome."

"This isn't the first time I've been in this situation."

"Name one." There was a bite to his words.

"I came to Earth in almost the same manner."

"Oh." He had never heard this story.

"My family tried to bring me home through illegal means as well. When they were able to contact me, I refused to leave. Earth was home by then. They couldn't find me for ten years." A sigh escaped them, and their body sagged. "My parental figure tried to pull me through. As I refused, it almost killed us both."

Brian's eyes went wide in terror. "Oh."

"Are you glad you didn't try to pull her through?"

"I wasn't..." he shook his head and stopped trying to deny the truth. "I wanted to pull her through so badly, but that's not how we are. We have..." he paused, and changed his language, "we always <u>used</u> to encourage each other to do our own thing, to be independent. We weren't two halves of a whole, we were two whole pieces navigating together on this messed up little rock."

"That's the best way."

Brian gave his friend a small, sad smile, then looked down at the papers in his hand. The paper was burgundy. He unfolded them gently, and saw yellow ink. As he shifted through them, he saw which ones were for him and which ones were for her parents. The paper was rough on his hands, but felt sturdy, like they wouldn't degrade anytime soon.

With the letters separated, he saw that the pile for her parents was twice as thick as the ones for him. A pang of jealousy ran through his body until he realized Bethany had written something to each of her parents and her two siblings. He sighed as he sorted the letters and folded them back up.

As he tucked the letters into his back pocket, he stopped, a quizzical look on his face. "Wait a minute." He looked at D'Azal. "Where's the bag of magic?"

"It dissipated when the portal opened. I told you that would happen."

Brian felt dazed. "I don't remember that part."

D'Azal's skin turned a particular shade of blue, which was what they looked like when they were laughing. "You said that a lot in the past year."

"I'm not sure what to make of that."

"It was interesting, nothing more."

"All right. Well, do you want to come with me to talk to Bethany's family tomorrow?" He frowned. "Or maybe the next day. I may sleep a lot. I'm exhausted."

They turned navy blue. "I've never met her parents. What will they think of a non-human, non-gendered, telepathic mage?"

"They don't care. Bethany's sister still calls you the blue octopus, though."

They turned a neutral shade of blue. "I've been called worse. I'll come with you." They paused as their skin turned a shade of blue Brian had never seen before. It was as dark as the night sky, but seemed to sparkle. "Would you like to get some food? There is a diner close by."

"You look different." Brian's head tilted to the side. "Are you asking me out on a date?"

"Would it be terrible if I did?"

Brian opened his mouth to speak, then stopped to think for a moment. "I don't know. Bethany left two years ago, but I just found out a few minutes ago that she's not coming home. I don't know if this is the right time."

The sparkle did not go away and seemed to catch an unknown light. "She did encourage you to pursue me."

He held up his hands. "I can't do this yet, D'Azal. Please leave it alone for the moment."

"Of course. But I am hungry, as I imagine you are. And the diner has coffee."

Brian grinned at the inside joke. The diner near the campus served two dishes with the name 'coffee'. One was the drink made from coffee beans. The other was spelled 'khovee', but pronounced 'coffee'. It was a long, flat fish with quills extending from its neck to the end of its tail fins. Even cooked, it looked like it could kill a person.

Khovee was baked and served with a delicate, floral sauce that brought out its natural flavors well, and was ridiculously delicious. It was a delicacy of Khwath, a realm that had a lot of connections to Earth. As the diner was the only place in town to get khovee, the visiting inhabitants of Khwath went there often.

Though both were popular dishes, if an unsuspecting patron asked for 'coffee' without specifying, they received both the liquid and the fish. It was a running gag, and always elicited laughter from the locals. If the unsuspecting patron tried both items, people in the diner cheered.

"Ok. Let's get coffee. Plate for me, cup for you."

D'Azal's skin turned a warm blue, with a bit of the sparkle left over. "Thank you for saying yes."

"Thank you for helping me with Bethany. And really, we've been friends forever. Who else am I going to cry to?"

The cephalopod stayed the same color as they started back to the car. Brian walked close to his friend and sighed in contentment as he felt a tentacle slip around his waist. He moved closer to D'Azal and took comfort from his friend as sorrow descended upon him. He missed Bethany, would miss her for a long time, but was glad she was where she wanted to be. With D'Azal's tentacle around his waist, Brian felt safe. The start of a smile appeared on his face as he realized he was where he belonged.

ABOUT CAT STARK

Cat Stark was raised in California and now lives in Illinois with her fiancé. She has finished numerous novels and can't wait to finish more.

She currently has 5 books available: *The Elven Prince*, *Enter the Maze*, and *The Grey House Trilogy* which consists of: *The Grey House, Inside the Grey House, Protector of the Grey House*.

Find her here:

Website: catstark.com

facebook.com/catstarkwriter/

Twitter & Instagram: @catstarkwriter

THURSDAY

BY AUTUMN ROSE JUDE SMITH

i wanted to shave my head last night
and i know what you're thinking
"why ditch that beautiful brown hair?"
it's an understandable statement of course
but i felt this undesirable
indescribable
ache
not in my chest or my lungs
not even my heart
i think it was my soul
something was off
has been off, i should say
this part of me (soul?)
was trying to get out
or kill me maybe
i don't really know
but it was screaming
wailing, for some kind of change
i got so excited
like i had taken some kind of drug

injected caffeine into my veins

and as i stood there

under flickering bathroom lights

i saw my reflection

it's been awhile, i keep most my mirrors covered

but God, she was beautiful

and then i crashed

the ache was gone but my limbs became numb

every part of me became limp

so i put the razor in the trash

and i fell asleep

knowing i was who i was supposed to be

ABOUT AUTUMN ROSE JUDE SMITH

Autumn Rose Jude Smith is a passionate writer from Rockford, Illinois. She embarked on her writing journey at the age of four, and it has remained her lifelong passion. With a history of multiple publications, Autumn's heart and soul are dedicated to poetry. Her writing delves into life's challenges, relationships, family, and the world around her. Autumn's mission is to elevate poetry within her community and amplify her unique voice.

FIVE SCENES FROM AN UNDECLARED RACE WAR

BY THOMAS L. VAULTONBURG

"It is the story of a school district that, at times, has committed such open acts of discrimination as to be cruel and committed others with such subtlety as to raise discrimination to an art form." -Judge P. Michael Mahoney Nov. 3, 1993 People Who Care Lawsuit.

2023. Rockford has a 72% minority public school enrollment and a 16% reading proficiency percentage.

Art Wash

a million vapid
murals won't teach kids to read...
or was that the point?

May 30, 2023

after the crackdown
old white men wander like ghosts
behind City Hall

Fourth Estate Sale

the only press left
is whatever ink hasn't
dried up in my pen

As Long As You're Not Dumb Enough
To Actually Try It (Summer 2020)

your clever free speech
zone implies the presence of
a non free speech zone

Rockford Summer 2023

police lights leave one
more Black man calling his Mom
with his final breath

About Thomas L. Vaultonburg

Thomas L. Vaultonburg was born in 1969 at Swedish American Hospital in Rockford, Illinois. For the last fifteen years he has operated Zombie Logic Press, and later Wolf Twin Books, with his creative partner Tre, on South 3rd Street, less than a mile from where he was born.

THE HANDS THAT MOVED HER

BY MEGAN ALBERTO

S he spread out the blanket and pillow she had on the carpeted floor of the old apartment that was new to her. It was dark and the electricity hadn't been turned on yet so she figured she'd get some shut-eye. But, when she closed her eyes, faces appeared – then spun around – distorted – then disappeared – only to begin the cycle again. She tried to squeeze her eyelids to make the images stop. She diverted her mind to thoughts of joyful moments, like the time she and her best friend Audrey had picnicked in the park.

At age fifteen they had packed up a basket of Lunchables, grapes, Bugles, and water (and a little something extra), before walking the mile and a half to the forest preserve at the edge of the neighborhood. The sun had been bright that day but a breeze kept it cool enough, and a dip in the creek made for the perfect afternoon. Audrey pulled a paisley patterned blanket from a tote bag and lay it across a grassy patch beneath a large old oak tree. The girls laughed easily with one another just as they had since meeting in the fourth grade. Charlotte had immediately admired Audrey's natural beauty and sense of humor. As a quiet awkward child, Charlotte felt at ease in Audrey's presence; Charlotte's intensity intrigued Audrey. Living just blocks from one another they'd been spending most weekends together for years.

Once Charlotte and Audrey finished the picnic they giggled as Audrey pulled a small plastic bag of mushrooms from the basket.

"These aren't too strong, right?" Charlotte had asked Audrey.

"No, no. Ryan said that if we eat three or four it would just make things a little more fun, but not crazy," Audrey reassured Charlotte.

"Hmmm. Okay. I'm still nervous."

"It'll be fun! Come on," Audrey pleaded. She held the bag open in front of Charlotte, waiting. Charlotte pursed her lips together before plunging her fingers into the bag and counting as she plucked. One, two, three. She held them in her palm.

"They look like they taste gross."

"I mean...we're not eating them for the taste," Audrey giggled.

Charlotte popped them into her mouth all at once and chewed, grimacing as she did. Audrey laughed as she watched. Charlotte pointed to the bag insisting that Audrey join her. Audrey counted four and popped them in, laughing and grimacing. The girls swallowed and then looked at each other.

"When is something supposed to happen?" Charlotte asked Audrey.

"I think it takes a little while." Audrey laid back on the blanket and looked to the sky through the oak branches that hung. Charlotte joined her and they watched the clouds as they waited.

The sun shifted position and ducked behind a cloud. A blue jay flew low and landed on a branch above Charlotte. As it did she let out a bellowing laugh that startled the jay away.

"What?!" Audrey demanded to know.

"I don't know!" Charlotte answered through continued laughter. "That blue jay just looked so...so...funny!" She cackled and began to roll around on the blanket.

"I don't get it!" Audrey smiled with confusion. Just then a fish jumped up from the creek and Audrey belted out a foghorn guffaw. "Okay, I get it now!" She thumped her hand on the ground.

The pair sat facing each other and asked what the other's pupils looked like. Charlotte gazed at Audrey and Audrey told Charlotte that she had always loved her dark curly hair. Charlotte told Audrey she hated it and had always wanted her auburn straight hair. Audrey looked to the right and swore she had seen a rabbit hop in the forest. When Audrey looked back Charlotte found herself leaning in and planting her lips onto Audrey's. Charlotte's lips tingled as she leaned back out and her body filled with warmth. Her eyes opened to find Audrey's eyes wide.

"Oh my god, I'm so sorry. I don't know what that was!" Charlotte exclaimed.

"No. no. It's okay. I mean, we're fucked up and just having our college lesbian experience a little early, right?" Audrey waved Charlotte off.

She'd forgotten how that joyful moment had soured. How it had in fact ended a five-year friendship just before their high school years. Her mind had betrayed her. And now she was lying on a carpet floor all alone, tears wetting her pillow.

Bright rays of sun hit her face through the curtainless windows the next morning. She pulled her pillow over her face, wanting to block out the demanding day. She'd told herself she'd need to find a job the next day and that day had come. Groaning, she pushed herself to sit and looked around the room. It wasn't a terribly small living room. She could see the eat-in kitchen from where she sat and the hall that led to the one bedroom and bathroom. Everything was white and beige. At nineteen she hadn't pictured herself living alone in a strange city, but not much in her life had been expected.

"Okay, I'll get myself dressed and ready. I've gotta look good. And, then I'll take that piece of crap Chevy out and see what I can find." Charlotte spoke aloud to herself.

"There's gotta be a job out there."

Her black and red duffle bag which she'd had since her soccer days in middle school was stuffed to the gills with as many clothes and toiletries as she could cram in during the twenty minutes she'd had to pack up. She found a white button-up shirt (a bit wrinkled) a nice pair of jeans, a bar of soap, and her make-up bag. After freshening up in the small but functional bathroom, Charlotte shoved her feet into her loafers and grabbed her keys. She looked at them for a moment – in near disbelief – that she'd managed to land in a place she could call her home – all hers. A pair of ruby slippers hung from the chain, a souvenir she'd picked up during a road trip in North Carolina her junior year. She'd begged her family to stop at the Wizard of Oz amusement park but after detouring for several hours they found the park had been closed up for many years. They'd found the remnant at a gift store not far from there that had taken advantage of the tourists who still came around to gawk at the abandoned park. Charlotte thought about her excitement and disappointment throughout that trip and sighed. She steeled herself for what could meet her that day.

Her first stop was a gas station, whose attendant told her briskly that they were not hiring. Next, she found a Burger King just down the road. She was given an application which she filled out on the spot, but when she told them that she did not have a phone number to call they told her to come back in on Friday to speak to the manager. "But it's Tuesday and I really need a job." She'd said. "Sorry." The young boy said. She got back into her Chevy and looked at the gas tank. Near empty. "Shit." She looked up and saw an Italian deli just up the street.

After the short drive, Charlotte took in a breath and put on her best smile for the woman behind the counter.

"Hello. I was wondering if you are hiring." Charlotte asked as pleasantly as she could manage.

"Actually, we just lost one of our best girls and we are looking for someone to take her place. What experience do you have?" a woman who later introduced herself as Linda said.

"I used to work the drive-thru at a Wendy's. I was their best employee. I just moved here."

"Well, when can you start?" Linda asked.

"Right now!" Charlotte nearly shouted, then caught herself. "Right now, ma'am."

"Well, don't go around ma'aming me and we'll be just fine." Linda smiled. She waved for Charlotte to follow her to the back room where she gave her an apron and an employee manual. She explained that the deli had been an institution in the Rockford area for decades and that they took customer service seriously. Charlotte nodded and remained attentive. Linda gave her a tour which included a wall of pictures of all the family members that had worked there over the years keeping the tradition alive. She was shown a recipe book that looked like it had been used since the deli's grand opening, the menu, and a run-through of how to work the cash register. She asked Charlotte to come in five days a week for six-hour shifts. Charlotte agreed to everything, knowing it would take at least that to make rent, let alone gas and all the other bills she would somehow need to figure out how to pay.

"When's your birthday?" Linda asked.

"October 4th, 1984," Charlotte responded.

"So, you're 19, huh? I would've figured 24. You carry yourself well." Linda stated.

"Thank you, ma'am. I mean... thank you." Charlotte smiled halfway. She'd heard this most of her life. Having to grow up quickly makes one –well –mature. It wasn't something she felt particularly proud of. "Is there any way I could work a shift today and get paid in cash? Like I said, I just moved here and my gas tank is empty. I hate to even ask. It would be the only time, I promise."

"I think we can work something out. Just for today." Linda looked sternly at Charlotte.

"Yes, of course."

Charlotte emptied out boxes and organized the storage, sliced tomatoes and peppers, learned how to make brine for olives, and co-ran the register for the evening rush. As the day came to a close she swept the dining room floor and washed dishes. Linda approached her with an envelope and told her she was glad to have a hard worker join their team, and to be back at 11 am the next day. Charlotte took the envelope and thanked Linda, fiercely.

The Chevy started up in the parking lot and took her half a block down the main road before slowing to a crawl and then dying. The gas light came on. "Fuck." Charlotte got out, locked the doors, and began walking toward the gas station a half mile away. She'd not gotten more than ten steps before she heard someone call out to her.

"Did your car run out of gas? Hop in! I'll drive you there." Linda called from her car.

"It's ok! I can walk!" Charlotte yelled back.

"Don't be silly! Get in!" Linda insisted. Charlotte considered arguing back with her but acquiesced instead. It'd been a long enough day and who was she to turn down help?

"So, where did you say you moved from?" Linda asked as they drove.

"I didn't. Just outside of Chicago." Charlotte responded.

"And, do you have family here?"

"Not really, just a few cousins that I don't really talk to."

"What brought you here?" Linda asked.

Geeze, she has a lot of questions. Is this my payment for the ride? "Um, I just needed to get away."

"Sorry. I didn't mean to pry."

"No, it's ok. You weren't prying." They pulled up to the gas station. Charlotte went inside, found the small gas canisters, paid for the gallon of gas meant to fill it, and a ham sandwich. She could audibly hear the growls coming from her stomach and tried to remember the last full meal she'd eaten. As Charlotte finished filling the canister she saw Linda waving her back over. She obliged, taking the ride back to her car. Once back at the station, she pulled just enough from the envelope to pay for three more gallons meant to hold her over the remainder of the week.

Her new old apartment was only three miles from the gas station. After making the short trek home and settling in on her living room carpet she pulled out the envelope. The sun had set, however, and she couldn't see what was left. She decided she'd put together a budget first thing in the morning. The labor had tired her body and mind enough that for the first time in weeks, she found sleep quickly.

As the sun rose, Charlotte's eyes opened. Her legs were cramped after having been pulled up into her chest most of the night, still in jeans. Her button-up shirt twisted into her armpits. She straightened her clothing and sat with her back on the wall. Grabbing the envelope and a pen that she'd stuffed into her purse from a bank years ago, she looked at the cash. She had $29.25 left after paying for four gallons of gas and a sandwich. Her car got 20 miles to the gallon and she was asked to work five days a week. She'd be driving a little over 50 miles over the next three weeks before she got paid so she'd go through a little over two and a half gallons of gas. So, she had about thirty bucks to buy food for the next three weeks. She hoped the city would leave the water on until she could afford to put it in her name. She'd seen a Dollar General not far from the deli. She'd stop there after her shift to buy Top Ramen to get her through.

She pulled another outfit from her duffle and headed into the bathroom. As she unbuttoned her shirt, memories intruded upon her mind. Large hands unbuttoning her shirt, sweeping her dark curls behind her shoulder, whispers in her ear. She slammed her hands on the counter and looked in the mirror. *"He's not fucking here."* Her voice was clear and even. Her heart pounded in her chest but she exhaled forcefully and slowly in an effort to take control. She opened the tap and placed her hands in the cold water. Looking at herself in the mirror again, she repeated, *"He's not fucking here."*

Charlotte finished dressing and freshening up, to the best of her ability, and went out to the Chevy to check the time. She couldn't be sure that the time on the oven had been set right, and after looking in the car she was glad she had trusted her gut. She reset it and then waited until 10:15 a.m. to drive toward the deli. She arrived over half an hour early for her second shift and Linda expressed her delight by putting her to work right away.

On Charlotte's third day of work, she entered the deli to find a new face behind the counter. Jess smiled and greeted her, asking what she would like to order. Charlotte smiled back and told her she actually had just started working there.

"Oh! My bad." Jess said.

"No, it's okay," Charlotte said back. "Have you worked here long?"

"Well, Linda is my mom's best friend and I've known her and this place all my life. But, I just started working here last year." Jess replied.

"Right on. I'm sure you'll be able to help me get better at all of this."

"Absolutely! I'm no pro but if you have any questions..."

"Thanks!"

Charlotte and Jess laughed through the day as they got to know one another. Jess had been born in Rockford and lived there with her family. Her dad had left her mom for someone else when she was two so it was just her, her mom, and her brother who was three years younger. Jess told Charlotte that she was dating a guy named Adam whom she loved but couldn't be sure if he was the one. He seemed to be hot and cold when it came to hanging out. Jess asked about Charlotte's life and family. Charlotte gave her the cliff notes on where she had moved from, her high school, and that she'd just moved out here. Jess was inquisitive and a good listener, so she asked more questions and wanted clarification. Charlotte grew quiet, unsure of how to respond.

"Shit, I'm sorry. I can be so nosey."

"No, it's ok. It's just such a long boring story. You really don't want to hear all of that."

"I mean...I'm here to listen, but you don't have to talk."

"Thanks." Charlotte smiled as she faced Jess. It had been a long time since she'd felt she could really open up and trust a friend. She wanted to believe Jess was someone she could do this with, but they'd only just met. They spent the next hour shelving cans of tomato sauce in the dry storage. Charlotte watched as Jess moved lightly and appeared effortlessly present.

At the end of the shift, Jess asked Charlotte if she wanted to come over to her house for dinner. Charlotte thanked her but politely declined. While driving home she turned the radio on for the first time in weeks. "Alive" by Pearl Jam pushed through the speakers and before long Charlotte found herself singing along – and then screaming along to the lyrics. In the middle of belting out, "I'm still alive - hey," she nearly slammed on the brakes while going 45 miles per hour as she saw – almost out of the corner of her eye – a red '95 Mustang heading the other direction. Her heart pounded wildly in her chest and her hands went cold as sweat dripped from her armpits. She took in a forceful breath and tears fell down her cheeks. *It couldn't be. There's no way.*

Her beat-up Chevy had been nearly crawling and a car moved up behind her and began honking. Charlotte's mind raced as she decided she would pull into the neighborhood on her right and throw him off, just in case. She turned right, then left, then right again, and then parked in front of a small ranch. She turned the car off and exhaled. In an instant, she was back in the white brick house, with Sam. He'd come home from work and asked who she was getting dolled up for. She'd explained she had plans to go out with two friends she had met at work. His accusations came flying at her along with his bulky hands around her neck. She'd have to wear one of the handkerchiefs she'd started collecting. One to match every outfit. She pleaded with him and reassured him that he was the only man for her. His eyes went dark and his jaw tightened. Sam no longer inhabited the creature that stood towering over her, nearly twice her size. She looked down, submissive to his power, in a subconscious attempt to deflate the situation. When his anger eventually diffused she collapsed onto the floor. She waited for the television to click on and the beep of the microwave – then the light snore from the living room recliner – before fetching her cell phone from their bedroom and calling her friend to tell her she would not make it to the bar.

Charlotte's body had nearly frozen and she struggled to pull her hands from the steering wheel. She shifted and stretched, moving through the stiffness, as she looked up and down the street for any sign of his Mustang. All clear. It took several minutes for Charlotte to reorient herself, remembering where she was and how it was she got there. The fog lifted and she noticed she had turned the radio off in the midst of her panic. She turned it back on and one of her favorite 80's classics came through, "Time After Time" by Cindy Lauper. Charlotte pulled the rearview mirror down so she could look herself in the eye, "You got yourself out, Char. You're not there anymore." She pulled in a deep breath, pushed the mirror back into place, and put the car in drive.

That night proved to be restless, but in time Charlotte would find peace with sleep again. On her first payday, she went straight to the bank and opened an account, the first she'd had in her name. She drove to the library and asked to use their phone and set up water, electricity, and gas in her name at the new old apartment. Then she took herself out for tacos to celebrate.

Throughout the next few months, Charlotte would continue to talk with Jess at work and then push herself to invite Jess to her old new apartment. She'd been embarrassed at first, given the lack of furniture and overall plainness, but she'd been stopping at the local thrift shops on her days off to pick up kitchenware, blankets, tables, and decor. She even found a couch and mattress for cheap on her third stop out. Jess seemed content to let Charlotte open up to her in her own time. It would be nearly a year before Charlotte would tell Jess about Sam, and two months more before she'd use her new cell phone to reach out to her parents whom Sam had alienated her from. She'd screamed at her mother that she was an abusive narcissist, something Sam had convinced her of. Upon hearing from her, Charlotte's mother maintained an air of distance. However, over time Charlotte told her more and more of what she had gone through with Sam – the manipulation tactics he had used – the violence – and she slowly reopened.

Jess had connected Charlotte to the local domestic violence support groups where she started to learn about the trauma she'd been through and why she'd felt like she'd been losing her mind and blamed herself for it. Six months later Charlotte asked Linda if she could hang a flier for the DV center in the deli and Linda opened up to Charlotte about her own experience. Moved and angered, Charlotte decided to take action and began volunteering at the DV center and enrolled in college classes. She wanted to learn everything she could so that she could help spread the word, let others know what to look for in abusive relationships, and let victims know they were not alone.

It took Charlotte seven years to finish her undergraduate degree while working at the deli, volunteering, and then later working at the DV center; all while taking classes and studying at night. The days were long and hard. Though it took everything she had she never lost her focus. She convinced Jess to work part-time at the shelter with her and they tag-teamed hosting game nights for the residents. Jess eventually moved into another new old apartment with Charlotte that had a balcony and vaulted ceilings. They would have friends over for drinks on weekends and gather for brunch on Sunday mornings. They held a standing lunch date with Linda once a week at the deli to keep her up to date on their shenanigans.

On graduation day she excitedly texted Jess and Linda that she had parked in the lot and would meet them after the ceremony. Her cheeks nearly hurt from smiling so widely. Giddiness rose from her stomach to her chest as she turned the car off, but the giddiness shifted to panic as she looked up and saw a red '95 Mustang. She could hear her pulse in her ears as the car door opened. But, she exhaled audibly as a slender high-heeled leg swung out from the car and a tall brunette in a red dress exited. "*He's not fucking here,*" she said to herself, this time with confidence and a little bit of sass.

Charlotte found her seat with classmates she'd grown to know and admire. Peers who had shared similar stories to her own. Some who had known others who'd lost their battle with abuse. They greeted her with smiles and excited embraces. As she sat she looked around the auditorium and took it all in; the frenetic energy in the air, the supportive friends and family finding their seats, and graduates in gowns rushing about. *She was fucking there*.

ABOUT MEGAN ALBERTO

Megan Alberto is a freelance writer and Mental Health Therapist. Megan has lived in the Rockford area for over twenty years and is a mom of two children. She enjoys writing stories that evoke emotion and explore the human condition. Her work can be found in Register Star Media, Rockford Parent Magazine, Substack, and Visible Magazine.

THE UNDERROCK

BY JP RINDFLEISCH IX

The Bookstore

The drive back to Rockford, with a car packed full of their things, was not a particularly exciting day for Riley Thompson. After all, returning to a place with so many burned bridges would not be an ideal situation for anyone. Even the weather was apprehensive, summoning nearly the entirety of Lake Michigan onto Riley's car the whole adventure home.

Perhaps it was their imagination, but they could see a gloom settled on Rockford, exuding a tangible shroud that dampened, pun intended, the city's vibrancy that Riley had remembered. Bold murals were now drained of color, statues distorted into monstrous figures through flooded windshields, and towering brick buildings stared down at them, waiting for the opportune moment to descend on Riley.

Amid this desolation, a store of labyrinthian literature held its ground. Riley killed the engine, light from the storefront streaming into their car, dredging up memories of poets and writers performing their works from within those walls, breathing life into the yellowed pages and faded ink. Even now, years later, it remained a lighthouse amidst the darkness, a place filled with a thousand unexplored worlds, each whispering their tales within their timeworn pages.

Riley grabbed their satchel, containing the most important thing within this jam-packed car, a manuscript they'd been working on for the better half of five years, and stuffed it under their cardigan and denim jean jacket. The tempest was in full force, and they nearly drowned before stumbling through the front doors of the bookstore, gasping for air.

As they wiped off their thick, black framed glasses and pulled off their dripping knit mustard yellow hat which covered a close cut shaved head, they heard a familiar, laugh and gruff voice.

"Aren't you a sight for sore eyes," George, who sat hunched over a dismantled teal Royal Classic Typewriter, said. Gray might have peppered his hair, but he was no different from the man Riley had remembered years ago. Even his choice of attire, a faded shirt that read, 'Can't Pay Bills with Thoughts and Prayers,' was a picture perfect memory.

"Uh, hey, long time no see," Riley said.

George picked up his small screwdriver and focused on his work, wiping grease off on his pants. "What are you lookin' for?" he rasped.

A knot formed in Riley's throat. It had been years since they'd talked with anyone from here, anyone that remembered, and for some dumb reason, they wanted to pull the bandaid off even before they stopped at their new home. Not even five minutes back, and they stood in front of one of their most honest critics. "I'm looking for something on self-editing."

George scoffed. "Could've used that a couple of years ago, eh?"

There it was, the verbal punch to the gut they were waiting for. Who knew publishing an article that may have put Rockford's creative scene in a bad light would have grabbed as much attention as it did?

But that life was behind them. "I've been sticking to fiction these days. Dragons, fairies, magic, and a little less commentary on home. It's actually been pretty cathartic, and—"

"Not fishing for a backstory," George cut them off. "Books on writing are in the way back."

"Got it," Riley said as they hurried on, past the counter and deeper into the store.

It was bigger than Riley had remembered, with rooms nestled into each other, and walls adorned with shelves of books. It was a literary haven. A place where all voices sang in harmony, from ancient pillars of literary renown, to unknown faces forming a blip on history.

Riley could spend hours here, running fingers along embossed titles and doorstop paperbacks. But, before they reached the last room, a cold breeze passed by, and the satchel at their side snapped, dumping the entirety of their manuscript onto the ground. Of course, the clip holding the pages together failed, and papers slid and glided across the floor.

They dove down to one knee, grappling handfuls of paper as the phantom breeze grew stronger. Their pages swept up in this strange tempest, and Riley was certain George would be rounding the corner any second. Yet, he didn't come, and the papers fluttered in the air like snowflakes, traveling deeper into the store.

Riley crawled after them, madly grabbing at the air, stuffing pages back into their bag, only for the pages to somehow fall back out and flutter around them. Of course, like any good writer they knew, this was the one and only copy of their work. Even the computer they'd written it on was long since gone.

Had they not been in a panic, they might have noted the walls stretching and changing around them. Shelves expanded from floor to ceiling, wrapped around corners, and crafting impossible archways.

The pages picked up pace, swirling around in a small tornado in front of Riley. One last page snapped out of Riley's hand, and the cyclone shrunk, pages balling up and curling around each other, taking the shape of a small human.

"What the..." Riley started, their head cocked sideways as this being stared back at them with inky eyes.

"Hi!" The thing said, its voice shrill and childlike.

Riley stumbled to their feet. "What? What the hell are you?"

The collection of papers inspected their arms, spreading fingers out and balling them into fists before placing them on their hips. "I'm your manuscript, Manny. Boy hero extraordinaire."

"Manny?" Riley said, backing into a shelf. They turned around, noting a shelf that wasn't there moments before. A shelf that stretched high up into a darkness. Riley's heart raced as they spun around in a room that was no longer a room, leading off into other rooms that were nothing like Riley had seen before. "Where the hell am I?"

"In the neither-here-nor-there," Manny said, cartwheeling over to a shelf of books and pulling out a picture book, which promptly left Manny's hands and fluttered up into the darkness above.

"Well how do I get back to here? Or there? Or wherever we just were?"

Manny shook his head so vigorously it spun completely around several times before stopping, then pointed at Riley. "You can't. Not yet. The UnderRock needs help."

"UnderRock?"

Manny nodded, his papery arms rippling and shifting until he held a paper sword and shield. "It's under attack, and you're its only hope."

"Okay," Riley said, inching away. "And if I wanted to get out of here, where would I—"

"No, wait!" Manny pleaded, paper weaponry receding back into his boyish shape. "I'm serious. I was sent to get you."

"I can't. I have to get back. My car is packed with my stuff. I can't just—"

"Please?" Manny asked, his eyes growing abnormally wide.

Riley looked past the shelves and into halls and corners that carried on into darkness. There was no clear exit sign, nor any indication on which way might lead them back into the bookstore. They were here, alone, except for this thing in front of them, which seemed to know something more about this place than they did. "Fine," Riley said. "Lead the way."

Manny smiled wide and waved them on. "Come on, we have to hurry."

They delved deeper into the labyrinth, turning sharp corners and walking through archways and bridges made from books. Had Riley attempted to travel this without their companion, they'd be certain they'd be lost, however, in no time they stepped into what seemed like an large amphitheater, with a copse of perfectly shaped pine trees resting in the center.

"Made it," Manny's voice rang out. He paused and turned around to Riley. "I can't tell you what to expect, but stick close to me and we'll be safe."

"Safe? From what?"

"Come on," Manny said, waving them on as he slipped in through the trees.

"Wait! Safe from what?" Riley said, chasing after him.

They slipped in between the trees, weaving their body left and right. They caught glimpses of Manny's leg or arm as they traveled deeper between the trees, which were clearly more dense and much larger than what they had seen in the amphitheater.

Gray light filtered in through the trunks seconds before Riley weaved out from the trees and out onto a rooftop, bumping into Manny.

The sky was no longer filled with dark clouds, and the rooftop was completely dry. Yet, the sky wasn't blue. It was gray, as was the sun, high up in the sky, a circle of gray, colorless light.

Manny turned around and smiled, arms stretched out. "This is the UnderRock, and it's dying."

The UnderRock

From the rooftop, Riley peered out into a distorted canvas of downtown. Below was State Street, without a doubt, but everything had changed and shifted. Buildings stretched and bent at odd angles, and the Rock River, which should have been out of view, drifted up in the sky, inky black waters dancing overtop the bridge. Beyond the buildings were strange ethereal flowers, taller than any skyscraper Riley had seen, appearing to be made of glass. It would have been a beautiful sight, had it not been for the lack of color. It was as if color had been leached away, and the longer Riley stared at the structures, the more cracks and crumbled stone they saw.

A resounding thud jolted Riley from their trance. They spun on their heels, spotting the first splash of color they'd seen in this otherwise bleak land that resembled an abandoned amusement park. The white hands that once shaped RKFD now clustered to one side of a painted mural filled with blocks and flowers of sunlit yellow and neon magenta.

The hands quivered within the mural, scratching and crawling overtop one another, desperately picking at the edge. As Riley watched, a singular finger broke free from the confines of the bricks, extending a fragile, paper-like digit out into the air.

Manny recoiled, pressing himself into Riley's legs, his gaze fixed on a point across the roof. His whisper was nearly inaudible, "We... we have to run."

Riley followed Manny's gaze and found a looming figure, draped in what looked like a robe of undulating letters. Long, pale, spider-like fingers scratched at the edge of the mural. With each stroke against the mural, the color sapped up into the being's hand, as if they were some kind of sponge.

"No point in running," the being hissed, voice dry and raspy.

Riley looked down at Manny, who trembled at their legs. "Who is that?" they whispered.

Manny turned and buried his face in Riley's leg. "That's the Grey Byline. Please we can't stay here!"

The Grey Byline's long fingers slipped into the walls, stretching and bending across the brick mural. Then, in an instant, fingers flashed across the wall and pierced through one of the hands. It wriggled, pushing at the razor-sharp spears that punctured it, before falling still. Paint flaked around the hand's edges, and the Grey Byline's fingers reared back for another attack.

"Wait, stop!" Riley shouted.

From within the hood, a face of marbled stone stared out at them. Had it not been for the ever growing glare, Riley would have thought it to be actual stone. It was beautiful in every way, as if carved by the finest craftsperson, with a smooth jaw and strong eyebrows.

Manny raced around Riley's legs, using them as a barrier.

The being smiled, pulling their hand free from the mural, stepping closer to Riley. "And who might you be?"

Riley puffed out their chest and glared back. "What are you doing to those hands?"

The Grey Byline smiled, entwining his spidery hands together. "These *hands* transgress the laws of this realm. The only proper thing to do is eradicate them."

"So you just kill them?" Riley said, glancing over as one of the hands nudged at their fallen fellow. "They're terrified of you."

The Grey Byline frowned. "You aren't from here." His eyes drifted down to Manny and he smiled. "You brought this...human...over?"

"Don't switch the subject!" Riley shouted. "What is wrong with you? Who died and made you king?"

A raspy laugh resonated from the Grey Byline. "Look around. Everything died, and I took what remained. Just like I'll take your friend."

The Grey Byline's fingers unfurled and stretched, shrinking the distance between them.

Riley acted on instinct, jumping back. But they miscalculated, and their legs rammed into the side of the rooftop, sending them over the ledge.

Their heart fell into their stomach as the sense of weightlessness overtook them. An inconceivably large hand swiped above them, missing them by a hair.

Was this it? Did they come into a strange world, only to fall from a roof and die?

Papers flittered past them, swirling around like some kind of storm.

They'd gone all this way, traveled back home to try and start things over, but here they were falling to their death.

Wait, not falling. Floating.

They frowned, turning their head left and right, realizing their descent had been slowed from a mass of papers, from Manny, who supported them as they glided down from the roof.

A blob of balled up paper formed a face in front of Riley. "We need to run! Before the Byline comes down. Before—"

Long fingers wrapped around the face in front of Riley, closing in and pulling Manny away. With it, flutters of papers drifted up from behind Riley and trailed behind the captured face.

With each page lost, Riley fell faster, until they dropped, landing hard onto solid ground.

Downtown

Riley groaned as they rolled over on the cold asphalt. They pushed themselves up, brushing off the dirt and debris and taking in their surroundings. An eerie, almost suffocating fog enveloped them and they couldn't see much farther than a block.

Somewhat familiar buildings, distorted and stretched as they were, now stood like skeletal remains, hollowed out and devoid of warmth and color. This place was somehow worse than looking at it from above. It was like Riley had fallen into a forgotten dream, thrown somewhere in the back of one's mind to wither away.

Silhouettes dipped in and out of the mist, trudging along the road mindlessly. Most of them were human forms, but from what Riley could see, they resembled washed out watercolor paintings more than actual flesh and blood. A few paused, hollowed out eyes locking onto Riley. As they did, more and more stopped, until a circle of onlookers stared at them.

A woman, well set into her curves with voluminous grayed hair, approached. As she shouldered through the crowd, Riley saw that the woman wore a gray blouse and pencil skirt, and silvered jewelry that glinted in the dull light. The woman cocked her head at Riley, looking them up and down before speaking in a smooth tone. "My aren't you vibrant?"

Riley frowned and looked down at their clothes. While they would say their mustard yellow hat and denim jacket were particularly vibrant, they supposed here, in this place, it stuck out like a sore thumb.

"Um, thank you?" They looked up, noting that the fog down here was so dense they couldn't see the roof above. "The Grey Byline. He's up there. He—"

The woman waved her hand and stepped closer to Riley. "Oh, don't worry, dear. The Byline wouldn't dare risk his letters running down here." The woman said. "You're out of his reach. For now, at least."

Riley shook their head. "But my friend. Manny. He took—"

The woman's face dropped, and a shadow of sadness flitted across her face. She reached out, and rested a hand on Riley's arm. As she did, color seemed to bleed into the woman, darkening her skin as it rose up her arm and added a faint blue into her blouse. "Then I fear your friend is lost. The Grey Byline doesn't give back what he takes."

Riley took a few breaths and looked around, taking in the weight of dozens of curious eyes staring at them. "Where—what is this place? And who are you?"

The woman squeezed Riley's arm, a faint red returning to the woman's lips. "Memories. Dreams. Aspirations. We're what's left."

"Left from what?" Riley asked.

The woman nodded up, into the fog. "The echoes of what the Grey Byline cast away."

"What is he?" Riley asked.

"Pessimism. Critique. The antithesis. He came here and fed on our joy and light, leaving behind these husks of what we once were."

The others surrounding them stepped closer, as if drawn in by the pale colors that seeped into the woman. Riley didn't pull away, something inside them knew this woman wasn't stealing the color out of malice, and it didn't seem to hurt Riley either. "But why is he doing this?"

The woman's voice softened, her lips turning a deep red. "To fit his twisted narrative. You saw that robe of his, yes? It's made from scathing words that made it into this world."

A shiver ran through Riley, and sweat formed on the back of their neck. They pulled away from the woman, pieces falling into place. "Manny said he was sent to get me. This Grey Byline. When did he first appear?"

"A few years ago."

"And Manny is my manuscript. And you're—?"

The woman smiled, and a warmth emanated off her. "I'm the joy and love that an artist poured into their work."

Riley nodded. "So, what we make above comes to life down here?"

"Yes," the woman whispered. "All of us are art and emotion, crafted by those above. Created to give life and beauty to this place."

"Then, I think I know where the Grey Byline came from," Riley said, their voice quivering. "I think I made him."

The woman nodded. "That's why I sent for you," she waved around in the mist. "This is all that's left, but you," she squeezed tight onto Riley's arm and the woman's hair took on a deep shade of black, and rich browns filled her skin while yellows replaced the silvered jewelry, "you have the power to retract them. To change the narrative."

Riley nodded. "I. I was in a bad place. I didn't know."

"The Grey Byline is powerful," The woman said. "But, if he is born of your words."

Riley nodded, "That means Manny is made from my words too. I have to save him. Where is he? Where can I find the Grey Byline?"

The woman pointed down the street, and into the fog. "The Grey Byline resides in the heart of the river of ink, within a building made of stars."

Riley grabbed the woman's hands, more color leaching into her. "I'll set things right. I promise."

The Star

Riley navigated the dense fog, passing by the shadows and echoes of murals, artwork, and faint inspirations from the creatives she knew from above. The closer they got to the river, the more they saw strange blobs of black liquid bobbing up and down in the air.

Light glinted out in the fog as the silhouette of a building, set out near the edge of the waters, came into view.

Whereas the blobs of black water seemed to hover all over the place, none of them seemed to approach this building. Each step forward was heavier and heavier, their past mistakes surfacing in their mind.

They stepped through the front doors, a marbled husk of a lobby, and inside, lay Manny, sprawled across the floor, more like a pile of papers than the small human shape he had before.

Riley kept their senses wide as they scanned the place left and right, looking for any sign of the Grey Byline as they approached.

"Manny?" They whispered.

Paper curled and crumpled into a face, weak and peering. "You came," Manny said.

"Of course they did," a voice said to their right.

Riley turned, and the Grey Byline sat, long spidery fingers interlaced, in a black chair.

Riley clenched their fists. "Let him go!"

The Grey Byline smirked and stood up from his chair. "I think not. He is mine. Just like everything else in this godforsaken place."

"I know what you are," Riley said.

"Oh?" The Grey Byline gave a slight bow of his head. He walked over to Manny, reaching a hand down. As he did, the pages reconstituted into the shape of a boy, laying still on the ground. "Then you know I have only you to thank for bringing me here and turning this place into your image."

Riley stared at Manny, his form unmoving under the Grey Byline. This was their fault. All of it. They breathed in, and said, "I wrote those terrible things, yes. I said hurtful things. Things that I didn't mean. I was wrong."

The Grey Byline grinned. "Yet I'm still here. Your regret can't stop the words already spoken."

Riley paused, breathing in for a moment, then said. "I know, but I recognize those words no longer reflect me. I let Rockford's imperfections tear a hole in me, but now I see the potential this place could have."

The Grey Byline stepped back, his smile wavering. "Your remorse can't save you."

Riley closed their eyes, holding the beauty of downtown in their mind. "But it's not remorse. I acknowledge what I did, and the destruction it caused. But this is the place that nurtured my creativity. When I left, I realized how much this place changed me."

The Grey Byline took another step back, their coat of letters starting to fray.

Riley continued, "For every broken window, there was an art exhibit. Every empty storefront was a new potential. We make the community we want to see, and if we don't show up, then the community dies."

With each word they said, the words off the Grey Byline's coat fell into a puddle of ink. The inky letters seeped into Manny, and the pages that made him up glowed.

The Grey Byline clutched at the remains of his robe, but as he did, the long spidery fingers receded, taking on a more human form. "How? What are you doing?"

Riley clenched their fists. "You no longer own my words," they nodded over to Manny. "He does. I can't take back what you are, but I can do everything I can to use my voice, my words, to speak of things that matter most. To speak of hope."

As the final words left Riley's lips, an explosion of color burst forth from Manny. For a moment, the Grey Byline stood, a stone statue in all its beauty, before crumbling to dust and flowing into Manny.

Manny clutched at his chest, growing a few inches taller as the pages all came together once again. He looked down at his hand, turning it over. "He's still in here."

Riley nodded. "I don't think he'll ever go away, but at least for now we have something better."

Manny breathed out, and with it, color came flowing out into the world. The floor shown with golden inlay, and the sofas turned a bright red.

They both smiled at each other, and together they stepped out into the UnderRock. Fog dissipated, the sky cleared, and the people walking the streets gained color once again.

Riley smiled, eying the murals as they waved back at them. "We did it," they said, turning to look at Manny.

But, instead of seeing Manny standing next to her, it was their manuscript in their hand, held together by a sturdy binder clip.

They looked around, wincing as the sun looked down on them. The people up and down the street weren't the strange and obscure art they had seen hours before, but people, stepping out after the rain had cleared. The art they could see didn't move, but instead brought a warmth to their chest.

They turned and looked at the storefront of the bookshop, catching George's eye.

They held on tight to their manuscript, happy they'd come home.

ABOUT JP RINDFLEISCH IX

JP Rindfleisch IX is the curator of things dark, strange, and queer.

Certified as a Three Story Method editor under the guidance of J Thorn and a Dialogue Doctor Editor within Jeff Elkins' community, JP's commitment to the craft is unwavering. Their works include *Mandrake Manor*, an LGBT Cozy Suburban Fantasy, *NRDS: National Recently Deceased Services*, a Paranormal Comedy co-authored with Jeff Elkins, and the *Leah Ackerman Series*, a Paranormal Academy Urban Fantasy co-authored with A.B. Cohen. Alongside these, their ongoing serial *Mosswood Apothecary* offers readers a dose of LGBT Cozy Fantasy.

JP has a firm belief that writing isn't a solitary venture. It's in communities, such as the one they spearhead with the Rockford Area Writers group, that JP believes writers truly flourish.

Inspired by a desire to see authentic representation, JP focuses primarily on crafting queer fiction—the stories a younger JP longed to read growing up.

To follow JP's journey and explore their varied works, visit: www.jprindfleischix.com.

CLOSERS

BY JONATHAN HANNEL

A 2009 Dodge Caravan pulled into the lot, then circled once through the inventory. *Not enough gross in the world to eat up that negative equity. Next.* Neil returned his attention to the solitaire game on his computer screen, made small enough to allow him to switch back the CRM program that the sales managers would expect to see should any one of the five of them pass his desk. Minutes later, a 2014 Honda Fit parked next to the Caravan; a young Indian couple walked through the door. *Too much work for a mini. Let the greenpea get his dick wet.* He continued aimlessly dragging and double clicking on cards, essentially letting the game play itself. For a moment, he considered following up on the leads in the CRM, but thought better of it.

Right on cue, Clark, sales manager #4 approached his desk. "Making your calls, Neil?" he asked.

"You bet, boss," Neil hadn't made any calls, but did log a series of "Call Attempt; No Answer" dispositions in the CRM.

"Great. Really gotta get people in the door. We want 100 new Hondas this month. We need you, buddy."

"Let's make it 120."

"That's what I'm talking about!" Clark extended a fist, and Neil casually gave him the bump. Neil returned to his card game, periodically looking out the window for the right opportunity.

Shortly after five o'clock, there were three cars on the lot: a 2004 Chevy Impala with no matching tires, a 2008 Honda Accord hauling a family of 5, and a 2013 VW Golf hovering over the luxury section of the used inventory. Neil walked directly toward the Golf, bypassing the credit criminal in the Impala and the family sure to want third row seating at at a two row price. By the time Neil approached his mark, the driver of the Golf, a twenty-something in tailored business casual, had already zeroed in on his car: a used 2016 Mercedes C-Class. Neil salivated at the prospect of a cock-sure young professional who had more budget than common sense. The only problem was the Benz; there wasn't much gross in it. The used car manager had offered too much when they took it in on trade, and the fair market value was hardly enough to cover the reconditioning costs. Neil would have to hold an extra grand or two on the trade to make a decent commission on it. Neil was confident that he could make it happen, but thought it best to flip the kid into the 2015, which was better equipped, similarly priced, and--most importantly--had about five grand of profit to work with. If Neil could get him at sticker while also getting the guy to accept a trade allowance less than its appraised value, he'd be looking at a monster commission, one that could pay off the outstanding balance on his youngest--and favorite--daughter's tuition bill that his ex-wife refused to split. *You wanted her to go to that hoity toity school, you pay for it*. Neil knew there was a way to get her to pay, but couldn't afford a competent lawyer to make it happen.

As the young man peered into the driver's side window, Neil made his move: "Just brought her in. Beautiful iddin't she?" Startled, the young man turned to Neil and nodded his head. "Neil Parkins. And you are?"

The young man accepted Neil's handshake and took his hand with a firmness that surprised him. "Connor Kemp. Nice to meet you." Neil was next supposed to ask if Connor had worked with another salesman, but always figured it would sort itself out later.

Neil didn't know shit about this M-Class, but also knew it wouldn't matter; young men never wanted to be told too much about cars. Instead, Neil just asked a series of obvious yes or no questions to which Connor could only answer, "yes."

"Iddin't that a sharp black finish?" Randy asked.

"Yes," Connor replied, without breaking his gaze at the car.

"Mercedes is all about fit and finish. Don't you love the detail on those alloy wheels?"

"Oh yeah."

"And look at that leather interior. All class, ain't it?" Randy finished, unaware of the irony in his diction.

"It really is."

Neil knew from his years in the business that the more you can get a customer to say yes, the more they begin to take mental ownership. Neil offered to take Connor for a test drive. Once Connor started driving, Neil shut up and let the car do the work. As they returned to the lot, Neil told Connor to pull into the "sold row." Of course, no such thing existed, it was just a couple of open stalls, but if Connor didn't object, he had taken mental ownership. Connor did as directed and put the car into park.

"So, how much is this one going for again?" he said.

"Thirty-five nine."

"How much do you think you can come off on that?"

"Unfortunately, I don't have a say in that. I do know they price these cars to sell though."

"Sure, but there's some room to come down, right?"

"If this is the car you want to take home tonight, I don't want price to get in the way. I tell you what, though, did you see that '15?"

"Well, I came here for this one. I'd like to see what you can do on this one."

"Of course. I'll get you the best deal I can. But how 'bout we take out the '15 and see which one you like better. It's a grand cheaper and comes with the luxury package. How 'bought we take her out and I run numbers on both?"

"Well, sure. I guess it wouldn't hurt to take a look."

While the differences were negligible, Neil played up the upgraded sound system, which seemed to be enough to tip the scales for this young hot shot.

"So what do you do, Connor?" Neil asked as he looked out the passenger window.

"Actually, I'm also in sales," Connor replied.

"Oh yeah? What do you sell?"

"Weight loss supplements. I mean, I don't sell them, per se. I'm more of a sales coach these days."

"Sales coach? Pretty impressive for a young man like you. How'd you wind up with that gig?"

"I started as a salesman a few years ago, hit it hard as hell. Made 100 grand in my second year."

"No shit?"

"No shit."

"Then I guess I'd better bring my A-game if you know all of the sales tricks."

"Naw, you're good. In fact, I appreciate the fact that you're showing me a cheaper car. I don't like when I feel pressured into the expensive shit by a salesman trying to get his nut."

Neil was relieved that the kid didn't know *all* of the tricks. "Well, that's my philosophy. I want to find the car that is the best fit for *you*. This car is certainly more your style, and I can get you a better deal on it."

"I appreciate that, Neil. I think I'd like to see what you can do on this one."

"No Problem. I'll get your Golf appraised right away."

Neil walked the kid to his desk and gave him a complimentary bottle of water, the only courtesy granted to customers spending thousands of dollars. He took the keys to the Golf and gave them to the used car manager to get the appraisal started. When he returned, he put the kid's information into the CRM. He'd not been claimed by another salesman, so Neil wouldn't have to split the commission.

Neil contemplated how badly he would rip the kid's head off. He didn't seem to put up much of a fight, but as the old dog in the used car office used to say, pigs get fed, hogs get slaughtered. He'd lost his share of deals by showing too high of an asking price, but Neil also knew that these types of deals don't come around often. This one deal had the potential to give him a lot of breathing room.

He went to the used car office to get the appraisal for the Golf, then took that and the other information into the sales office. Dan, sales manager #3, was ready for him. "Neil, do you realize how much gross is in that Benz?" He asked.

"Oh hell yeah. I flipped the kid from that '16."

"So how you want to play this? This kid gonna needle you, or do you think you can get him on the first pencil?"

"Well, the kid is a salesman, but I don't think he's the type to put up much of a fight. He wants a little discount, but I don't think he's gonna grind me down."

"Does he have any expectations for trade value?"

"I don't think so."

"Excellent. Alright, so let me know what you think of this: His Golf was appraised at 20k. Let's hold two grand on the trade and show him 18. Then we'll take a grand off the Benz. You think he'll go for it?"

"I'll see what he can do."

Neil took the negotiation paper and took a moment to collect himself. Holding two grand on the trade while only taking a grand of the new car meant that Neil would be looking at a 6 grand gross. From that, he would get a $1,650 commission, a once-a-year type of deal. This is where Neil shined. He could hardly be bothered to peel his pleated Dockers from his office chair to take an up and he never made cold calls, but if there was a guy that could close a deal in one pencil, it was Neil. The kid was a mark, but he couldn't over play it. He needed to give off the impression that he and the kid were on the same level, make the kid feel like he'd already won the negotiation. New guys could never be trusted to attempt something like this because they'd already come in their pants before hitting the desk. This was what Neil was born to do.

"Alright, Connor," he began as he took his seat, not yet revealing the negotiation form, "so here's the deal. Normally, how we do these things is we start with sticker price and then whittle it down a hundred or so at a time. But you're a fellow sales professional, so I don't wanna fuck around. I asked my boss to just do the best he could so we don't waste your time. Here's what we can do for you." He slid the paper across the desk and set the pen on top of it. Connor looked at it for a moment, then punched some numbers on his iPhone calculator.

"Anything more you can do on the trade?" he asked.

"That's really out of my hands. We've gotta be able to make something on it to make it worth our while, and the VW's have been a tough sell with the emissions scandal."

"For sure. I get that. It's just that I'm not totally sure I want to trade it."

Neil's heart sunk. Without the trade, he'd lose 2k gross, which would mean a 600 dollar cut in his commission. He had to keep it on the deal. "No problem," he said, "We can always take it out of the deal, but my boss gave you the discount on the Benz expecting that we would have a car to make some money to offset our loss, so we might have to kick up the price five hundred or so."

"Hmm. Yeah, that makes sense. Alright. What do you need from me then?"

"Just a title, a check, and a few signatures, starting with one right here."

Connor looked at the negotiation form one last time, then took the pen Neil offered, and signed his name, agreeing to terms.

"Congratulations, young man. You just bought yourself a Mercedes Benz. Not a whole lot of guys your age can say that in this town."

Neil took the signature back to the sales manager's office, refraining from smiling in order to act like this was an everyday sort of deal. He set it down on Dan's desk. "Write that bitch up," he said. Dan gave him an are-you-fucking-serious look and then wrote up the sales contract, printing out the rest of the paperwork as he wrote on the triplicate form. Neil returned to his desk with a stack of papers.

"Alright, we just need your signature a few times, and then I need you to fill out the credit app," Neil said as he placed the folder of papers on the desk.

"Oh, I don't need to fill out the credit app. I'm paying cash," Connor said, still staring down at his Instagram app.

"No shit?"

"Yeah, I figure, why take on the interest, right?"

"Damn, you must be killing it."

"Yeah, NutriSlim has been good to me."

"I guess so. So how did you get into it?"

"I had a buddy start selling it after college when he couldn't find a job. Started making bank, so I asked him to hook me up."

"So how does a person get into it?"

"Well, it takes an initial investment, but the stuff sells itself. My friends used to give me shit, saying that it was a pyramid scheme, but you can call it what you want. I'm on track to do 300k this year, and all of those friends who used to make fun of my pyramid scheme are working under me now."

"300? Hot damn. If you don't mind me asking, how come you're looking at used cars?"

"I just bought a house. Cash. So, I didn't want to take on too much at once."

"You bet. So what kind of time commitment does it take to sell that stuff?"

"Depends on how much you want to make."

"You said investment. How much are we talking?"

"Well, to start off, you need to buy our starter package. This will give you the tools, training, and products to hit the ground running. It's a little under 700 dollars, but if you sell all the products that come in that initial package, you double your money."

"So am I selling the product, or trying to add team members?"

"Right, the pyramid scheme thing. It's multi-level marketing. NutriSlim has found that word of mouth through social media is much more effective than traditional advertising, so they'd rather put their marketing money into the hands of our team members, the ones who are putting it out there."

"So does this shit work?"

"Neil, you wouldn't believe it. For real. I was never obese or anything, just always a little chubby. Now I don't want anybody getting the wrong idea, so I won't take my shirt off, but if I did, you'd see that it works. And if you want, you can ask her." Connor slid his phone over to Neil. On the home screen was a picture of Connor standing on the beach with his arm around a perfectly sculpted blonde.

"Damn, she's beautiful! Oh to be young again. When I was your age, I had'em lined up."

"I bet you did, Neil. Anyway, I don't want to push this on you, but I have to tell you that I liked your approach. I think you'd be a good candidate to join the team part time if you want to try it out."

"Shit, if you're making money like that, I might just have to."

"Great. Give me your email and I'll send you some info."

Carl, the finance manager finally made his way over to Neil's desk with the paperwork in hand. Neil could tell that Carl wasn't happy with the deal, which was typical of finance managers who took cash deals. Cash deals meant no backend for Carl, unless he was able to tack on a 3000 warranty. It's a hell of a lot easier to break that 3000 down into 60 payments for a finance customer, where he could present it as just a few extra bucks a month. Neil didn't give a shit; Carl made enough money.

As Neil waited for Connor, he opened the email Connor sent with the NutriSlim information. It looked like every other MLM business that he'd seen. He'd made a few bucks on some and got burned on some others, but if this kid really made what he said, this could be a sweet side hustle.

Then again, how did he know the kid was for real? Yes, he was currently writing a check for twenty-five thousand dollars, but Neil knew what it was like to be a young hotshot. You only spend enough to get laid: cars, clothes, dinners, whatever it takes to be somebody. Neil himself had lived in a dump as a young man, but would romance women with extravagant dinners and nights at hotels, racking up charges on a card that would hopefully be paid off with the next month's commission. But even if the kid was not exactly what he said he was, Nutrislim could still make him some extra cash. If he could just make an extra thousand a month he would be sitting pretty.

Soon, Connor emerged from the office, paperwork in hand. Neil greeted him offering the usual post sales service, "Congratulations, Connor. I got her washed and gassed up out front. How about I walk you through the features and get your phone connected?"

"That's alright," Connor replied, "I'm taking the girl to the city, so I gotta run. But I really appreciate how easy you made all of this. And again, I really hope you'll consider joining the team."

"I might just do that. Take care, and enjoy. And let me know when you wanna get the lady something nice."

"You bet, Neil."

The kid got in his new car and drove away. Neil looked at the clock and saw that it was 6:40, which was close enough to 7:00 for him to leave without being hassled by the Dans. It was bowling night, after all. When he got home, his house was empty. Sonja was working second shift at the gum factory and would meet up later. Neil poured himself a Jack and Coke and lit a cigarette. When both were finished, he took a shower, packed up his balls, and drove his 2005 Honda Pilot to Don Carter Lanes, Rockford's premier bowling alley, one complete with a two story bar, an arcade, and an off-track betting window. On the drive, Neil considered throwing a few bucks at the ponies, but remembered his daughter's tuition. She wasn't in danger of getting kicked out of school, but the longer he waited, the greater chance of an embarrassing situation in front of her classmates whose parents had no problem with the tuition bill. He wouldn't play the horses tonight.

Ron was already placing his balls in the rack when Neil arrived. Neil and Ron had known each other since high school, which was not uncommon in Rockford. They'd drifted in and out of each other's lives, but the two saw each other through their most trying periods, the divorces, Neil's always present and occasionally severe gambling problem, Ron's alcoholism. To Neil, Ron was his bowling buddy, one to share some laughs and memories. Ron was a solid bowler, though he didn't hold a candle to Neil's accomplishments on the lanes, accomplishments that included four perfect games. While Ron had done a much better job of distancing himself from his demons in recent years, finding God and a good woman whom he would not divorce, Ron looked up to Neil. Here at Don Carter Lanes, Neil was the man.

"Hey there, old man," Ron called out to Neil, looking up from the rack.

"Ready for the big night?" Neil said, alluding to their face off against their only true competition in the league.

"You know it. Lanes are looking good tonight."

"They always are." Neil never felt more comfortable than when he rolled on these lanes. He knew just where the grease let up, the exact point that his ball would break. Though he'd bowled on hundreds of lanes in his life--including his yearly pilgrimage to Reno for the big tournament--all of his perfect games came at Don Carter. He'd never sniff a perfect game in Reno because he didn't have that intimate knowledge of the grease pattern, and he would consistently fail to even come close to his average. Don Carter would never host a tournament with a promise of a big purse, but it was home, and there, Neil was somebody.

"Make any big deals today?" Ron was always curious about Randy's work, despite his own job at the aerospace plant carrying infinitely more prestige and double the money. No matter how reviled a car salesman is, no matter how badly people have been burned by shady dealership practices, people are forever fascinated by them.

"Oh yeah, buddy. Some hot shot kid came in on a used Benz. Tore his head off. Kid had money to burn though. Makes a killing selling this weight loss supplement. Pulled in 300 grand this year."

"No kiddin',"

"Oh yeah. Hell, I'm thinking about doing some work for him, myself."

"Don't tell me it's one of those pyramid schemes."

"More or less, but Ronny, you shoulda seen this kid. Livin' the dream."

"Yeah, well let's see where that kid is in a few years after a new fad hits the street and he can't find any more suckers."

Neil knew that Ron had a point, but Ron wasn't a salesman. He had the fear. You don't last long in sales if you have the fear. People with the fear are too busy looking for reasons why something won't work out. The dealership brings in new guys at a three per month clip, and most of them have the fear. They have every reason why they shouldn't close the deal, why they shouldn't try to make as much money as possible. Neil was a salesman. He jumped on opportunities. He took risks.

Still, Ron's words stuck with him. He placed his balls on the rack and walked to the bar to order their usual drinks: a Diet Coke for Ron and a double Jack and Diet Coke for himself. Waiting for the bartender, he couldn't help but resent Ron's comment just a little bit.

He knew that he had played the part of a sucker in the past. He'd gambled and lost on his own used car shop in Loves Park. He'd grossly miscalculated the viability of a life with his first wife. But that happens. People call you a sucker until you hit it big, and then they don't say shit. Neil knew there was no guarantee in this NutriSlim game, but there was no denying the potential.

Still waiting at the bar, he felt his phone vibrate in his pocket. Opened it up and saw he'd received an email:

Hey Neil, it's Conner. Just wanted to thank you for your help. Meant what I said earlier too. I could use a guy like you on my team if your looking for some cash on the side. I got a promotion right now for our gold package. It's not something I usually recommend, because it's a bit too advanced for our new reps to take right off the bat, but I think you can handle it if you're ready to fuck. Normally the package lists for 2,899, but if you enter the code PerkinsGold then you can get it for 1,599. This package has the Glenn Gary leads, you know? You also get 5 times as much product. Most importantly, if you can move it all, you're looking at a take home of 15k dollars. There's so much markup in this stuff, but people keep buying it. If you're interested, all you have to do is submit your order to our website. And you can take as much time as you want, but I do have to let you know that I only have 4 codes to give, and it's kinda a first come, first serve sort of thing. Wish I could get more, but I don't make the rules. I've offered it to a handful of other people, but I'd really hope you consider, because I think you have a better chance of selling it than them. Anyway, whatever you decide, it was great working with you. Good luck with your bowling league!

Neil saw through the kid's tactics, but he didn't mind. You've got to create a sense of urgency to close deals. After closing the email, he checked his balance in his bank account: $1,987.45. He had a little wiggle room if he wanted to pick up the gold package. He wasn't going to say shit to Ron about the offer.

He returned with the drinks and saw that the Steves had arrived. Their team of four was ready to roll. The Deadwood Hookers, their competition, were also ready. The teams shook hands, preparing for the start. There was no bad blood between the teams, as they had all, at some point, been teammates in other leagues. Regardless, this was a big match, and there was a healthy competitive spirit between the two teams. Neil, still high off of today's big deal, was pumped. He carried that momentum into his first game, scoring a game-high 254.

He'd found his rhythm and was settled in, so he felt confident enough to order another drink. Normally, he'd order a double on his first and then go back to singles so that he wouldn't lose control. Tonight, he'd get one more double before reverting back to a more conservative drink. Ron didn't notice, and probably wouldn't have said anything if he had. It wasn't unusual for Neil to over-indulge, and when he did, Ron was always willing to drive him home if Sonja was unable. Neil's second game betrayed no hint of inebriation, coming in at 248. Through two games, Neil's team, The Turkey Club, had built up a very healthy lead over the Hookers.

The teams agreed to take an extended break between the second and third game, allowing them for bathroom and smoke breaks. Neil took the opportunity to do some research on NutriSlim, on the gold package, and even on Connor. The site looked legit, not some fly-by-night operation like the usual pyramid scheme. Through other websites, Neil perused a series of testimonials from both customers and reps, most positive, though some reps expressed disappointment at being unable to move the product that they had paid for. Neil saw these complaints as no different from the many who try and fail to sell cars at the dealership. They have the fear.

The most encouraging bit of research came from Connor's Face-book page. It was littered with pictures of him and his girlfriend in exotic locations, even videos of him speaking at sales conferences before hundreds of people. You can't fake that, Neil figured. Neil navigated back to the NutriSlim website, where he found the list of products. There they were, just as Connor said. He started doing the math in his head. He needed to write a tuition check before the end of the month so that the school would not withhold transcripts as his daughter began applying to colleges. Fortunately, he had the big deal coming through, not to mention other smaller deals that would be funded before the next payday, only two days away. If he wanted to order the gold package, he would have to live off of a couple hundred bucks for the next two days. No problem, he figured. Knowing there were only a few minutes before the 3rd game, he removed his debit card from his wallet, and entered his information to claim his very own gold package. Feeling alive, Neil ordered another double, ready for the final game.

Neil woke up the next morning on the couch, which was often the case when he came home drunk. He knew they didn't fight, as Sonja, a survivor of many of her own toxic relationships, never minded Randy's drinking as long as he was nice to her, but she couldn't handle his snoring when he would fall asleep drunk, so she would tuck him into the couch. Neil couldn't really remember getting home. He began to work backwards through his memory. The last thing he remembered was shooting pool at Shooters. Then he remembered winning the match, and then he remembered placing his order for the gold package. He felt a bit sick to his stomach when he remembered how much money he'd spent, but was still encouraged about what it could mean for his future.

Sonja entered the room with a cup of coffee and three Tylenol pills. She, a heavy drinker in her own right, was the greatest hangover nurse Neil had ever known. She never made him feel guilty about his bad decisions, mostly because she would be making her own when her Friday night--which was actually Friday--came. "Musta been a good one. Feeling ok, hun?" she said.

"Been worse," Neil mumbled. "Had to celebrate. Real nice deal yesterday."

"Oh? Finally gonna be able to take me back to Vegas?"

"One day. Gotta take care of that tuition check."

"Babe, I love you for doin' right by your kid, but I can't wait til you don't have to pay that tuition no more."

"I know, baby. Just wait. Things are gonna pop, and then we can go to Vegas, or Fort Meyers, or any of them places you wanna go."

"Mmhmm."

Randy meant it. As soon as he could take care of his debt, the tuition, and maybe college, he was going to give Sonja the world. He got up and joined her in the kitchen, where she was making a breakfast of scrambled eggs, toast, and bacon, a combination that somehow always felt like a special treat, even though Sonja made it three times a week.

A few hours later, Sonja left for work. Neil was feeling much better, but still didn't have much energy to do anything. He was happy staying in the house, maybe watching a movie or two. As he was scanning the channels for something to watch, his phone vibrated on the coffee table. It was work. *Fuck.* Normally when work called on his day off, that meant a customer he'd worked with showed up unannounced. He would either have to show up within an hour, or the deal would go to someone else, and he would have to split it. He had no intention of coming in, but he still answered the call to make sure they wouldn't fuck up his deal by giving the customer to a greenpea.

"This is Neil," he answered, as if there would be somebody else answering his cell phone.

"Hey Neil, it's Carl. I need you to do me a favor."

"I ain't coming in. I'll split whatever I've got in there, just don't give 'em to Jon. Kid can't hold gross for shit."

"Huh? Oh, no, you don't have anybody coming in. I'm just working on getting all the deals funded, and I need something from your deal yesterday."

"The kid?"

"Yeah, Connor. I kinda fucked up. I forgot to get the kid to put a signature on the credit app."

"Credit app? Kid paid cash."

"Well, he gave a down payment, but had a change of heart and decided to finance most of it."

"Why the fuck would he do that? Kid's rolling in it."

"I mean, I guess."

"What do you mean? He pulled 300k last year."

"Did he tell you that? Yeah, he was blowing smoke up your ass. Big talker, that one."

"The fuck you talking about?"

"Don't get me wrong, he does pretty well for himself, but he made a little under ninety thousand this year. I guess he did say that there was some big payday coming or something, but yeah, not exactly Donald Trump."

"Fuck."

"Oh, no, you're all good. The deal's gonna get funded. He's pretty overextended on credit--couple cards pushed to the limit, but he always pays on time, so I didn't have any problem getting it done."

"Well that's good, I guess."

"You guess? You're looking at a monster commission on this one. Don't worry."

"It's just that... well, never mind."

"Alright. Well if you could just have him stop in, that would be great."

"Yeah, no problem, Carl."

Neil hung up and tossed the phone back on the coffee table. He considered calling the bank to see if he could stop payment on his gold package, but didn't give in to the fear. Goodfellas was on AMC.

ABOUT JONATHAN HANNEL

Jonathan Hannel, a full-time teacher and part-time writer, has had his work featured in Points In Case and Morning Moot, although he often uses a pseudonym to avoid potential accusations of indoctrination from concerned parents. His dedication to both teaching and writing shines through his contributions.

A Poet's Manifesto

by Ryan Burritt

Come and let me show you the seeds of revolution

Thoughts written

It does not matter the tongue or dialect

Revolution is a manuscript

A treaty nailed to a door

A manifesto to inspire the downtrodden

A revolution is ideas turned to words

Because syllables can be smuggled

Paragraphs can be hidden

But most important

Words inspire.

Our histories are written

Our laws are written

And to fix those

Our amendments are written

A painting can cause emotion

But words can cause a spark

So come and see what causes revolution

And I will read it to you.

ABOUT RYAN BURRITT

Ryan Burritt is a poet out of Rockford whose work focuses on themes that affect his personal life. Themes of love loss and drinking, along with any other musings, become intrusive thoughts.

PEACE, LOVE, AND WHATEVER

BY DAVID W. PEDERSEN

The principal at Beauford Elementary was more plastic than stone. What I mean to say is that his life hadn't been carved out from any sort of real-world experience but had been molded to conform beforehand. He was propped up on bones without gristle and levelled out with no visual rasp marks or sanding. There was no grit to his character or substance to his vocabulary, no accent, no scars. His hands probably didn't know how to make a fist. When he spoke, silent words peeked out from behind his bleached teeth. He didn't stammer or hesitate or reach to make conversation, but his corporate language was intentionally difficult to follow, but none of that mattered because I had tuned out as soon as I realized that the talk that we were currently having wasn't a "good" talk.

He was lecturing me on budget cuts and logistics and the teachers' union and the board of trustees, and fiscal conservativism, and bootstraps, and the tightening of the regional purse strings, and deficits, and the fifty-year-old boiler that needed repairs, and the new outdoor track that held water after it rained, and various issues of public service that I wasn't directly connected with. I examined the room for visual liberation and was greeted with a dusty, IBM Seletric typewriter, a few stock certificates of appreciation, and a diffused glamor photo of a women done up with a Pentecostal bouffant, smiling in front of faux-marble backdrop. Useless information. All of it. Bland as a bucket of mulch.

"Carl," he interrupted my nomadic thought with a rehearsed professional tone, dear god let this be the end of his yammering. "Do you understand what I'm saying?" I understood, alright. It was a new year, at the beginning of a new decade, nineteen and ninety-one, and I was out another gig. This was the end of the road for me at Beauford—one of the few remaining paying venues for a folk singer in Rockford, maybe the region, probably the State of Illinois at this rate. Last year, it was the summer camp appearances and a handful of rec centers that dried up, then went the high schools, followed by the middle schools, and so on, and so forth, and whatever.

"I understand," I said, obviously lying. A calculated paw was placed on my jean-jacketed shoulder. "No hard feelings," he said, "We're all feeling the pinch right now." His hand was then removed and extended, which implied that I should be standing, and if I were standing, I would be walking, and if I were walking, I would be exiting his office for the last time. Clean. Cut. Inorganic. Premeditated. Precise. Where was this guy when JFK was killed? Probably behind the scope. I moseyed.

The halls of Beaumont Elementary were free of lockers and painted the color of mint chocolate chip ice cream. The tile beneath my moccasins shrieked with a thousand years of buffed wax. The case of my Gibson J-45, swinging, cast long shadows down the hallway and dipped in time with my impatient, flat-footed rambling. No 'Nam for this revolutionary. Hallelujah, thank the lord for these inferior digits, as much as they burned during hard times, in-betweens, postponements, and lengthy stands. Poor people are always the ones you see standing in crowds, and at that exact moment, bebopping through Beaumont, I wondered how many minutes of my life had been spent standing or waiting for some rich bastard to hand me the bad news. Plenty—that much was gospel. But not this time. *He* had been the one left standing. A smile cracked across my stupid mug. Onward to implosion. Left. Right. Left. Right.

It was all quiet on the Midwestern front. The revolution was over, ushered in by a melon-headed actor President, and New Wave, and Wall Street brokers, and John Rambo, and vinyl siding, and herpes, and then another melon-headed scarecrow CIA President followed by rock cocaine, and *Operation Desert Whatever-The-Shit*, and *The Ninja Turtles*, and the Dodge Caravan. We've lost the war and it was a forfeit, brothers and sisters. We handed this green earth to concrete men with steel umbrellas who sold it back to us for a piece of shade. Time to pack it in and move on out. Commencing *Operation Bug-The-Hell-Out*. Where do we go from here? Where can anyone hide when every place is exactly the same? This ain't my world no more but I've got no other world to dig into. Successfully knocked off my patch without as much as an increase in volume or a shot across the bow. Smooth. Level. Precise. In '68 they blinded us with chemicals in Chicago, and split our youthful minds with batons, and now here I was, twenty plus years down the line, agreeing to see myself out like a fly through a broken window. The new American standard. Building walls around your piece with the assumption of keeping *them* out, all the while you're boxing yourself into a place where *they* want you to stay—as far away from *them* as possible.

This thought was starting to get me fired up. If I was any sort of genuine revolutionary, I would halt my retreat, turn around, guitar in hand like a bar gunner at Iwo Jima, and show that constricted principal asshole exactly what it feels like to be on the ground at a rodeo, but here we are, man. Here we are again, Carl. Same story, same day, same place, same universe, same soul, and brother, the only thing that's constant about this place is change.

I hesitated in front of a classroom window—an ancient mirror. Staring at the children, I must have looked as if I were seeing my own ghost right about then, and I would almost testify that I did see my younger self sitting there, just then, in that room, sitting crisscross applesauce on my own island of shaggy carpet, watching with those same dark eyes I wore as a child—eyes that then stared back at me from a place in time when all was well and possible—living in a land with no doors, or fences, or gates. Only windows. In youth, the world appears to us as a road with no end. And time, being the duplicitous assassin that it is, is always slinking behind you. And as you drift down the road, further and further, time pulls itself inward with every experience. And the further you drift, the more time cannibalizes and consumes itself, lessening, more and then more and then more, and before you know it, there never seems to be enough time left over for anything of real substance and you're finally faced with the realization of a permanent end, and you understand that nothing you've done, can ever be undone—the road only heads one way.

"Carl?" The class sat silently and watched Ms. Petrie interrupt my existential gawking. "Have you come to play a song for the class?"

I had.

Unwillingly and unbeknownst to everyone at Beaumont, myself included, I had come to play and sing for these children one last time. There will be no exchange of worthless currency for this performance, but the show wouldn't be on the house—they will pay me with their time, and I will, in turn, attempt to carve a philosophy within their souls using Guthrie, and Seeger, and Dylan, and Van Ronk. And together, only together, can we unmask and unmold. I will sing deep and infiltrate the plastic lives in which they were being raised. I will breach the force-feeding of marketed material goods, and greed, and violent cartoons, and isolationism, with songs of community and sharing, in hopes that something can reach them larger than any corporate spell. I will reach into the well of their hearts and give them the only thing I have to give, which just so happened to be my most valuable possession—I will give them my fleeting time, the end of the road at Beaford Middle School, and all that I ask is for them to sing along. Noisily, and boisterously, and out of key. Together.

ABOUT DAVID W. PEDERSEN

David W. Pedersen is an author and poet from Rockford, Illinois. His work has appeared in the *Cold Hard Type* series by Loose Dog Press, and the *And Then* anthology by Chicago's Agitator Gallery. He is the owner of Rockford independent bookstore, Maze Books.

FOLLOW THAT GOOSE

BY WREN MEDINA

I took a little walk
down by the Rock River
and a silly little goose
did say to me:

You can't find happiness
wandering State St. Target when there's
not enough money
to make ends meet.

So, I took a little walk
down to where the sidewalk stops
and a silly little goose
did say to me:

You deserve love, my dear
and it can be found near
if you would open your eyes
to the power of community.

So, I took a little walk
to support my local mom and pops
and a silly little goose
did say to me:

Don't give up on your dreams -
compassion is revolutionary
when you band together to
unravel greed at its seams.

ABOUT WREN MEDINA

Wren Medina (*they/them*) is a transplanted Rockfordian who hopes
to continue the growth of revolutionary community spaces through
compassion for the human experience, building mental health and
disability awareness, and maybe a laugh or two.

Pagan Revolution

Patrick J. Murphy III

~Part One~

Mickel raced down dark, interwoven campus paths, his black robes mopping up the damp grass's midnight rain. Glowing orange light offered little solace on this night, as he took the final bend and spotted the solitary curving stone of Adams Hall Arch. The others were all already there. Thirteen cloaked figures, just like himself, except for what was underneath, all waiting. For him.

From the dilapidated arch strode the man that had brought them all together, Magnus Lightfoot, the leader of the Unseen Council stood tall with black flowing hair and silvered adornments on his cloak. Mickel took his place and the others shifted, ready for the ceremony to begin.

His voice rang out loud and clear: "Brothers and sisters gathered from the wards I welcome you. Tonight, we will change the world."

Murmurs whipped through the gathered crowd.

Magnus held up his hands, "Don't worry. All of your questions will be answered at the right time. But the hour grows nigh and we must make our pass into the next world." Mickel leaned forward, watching as Magnus reached into his cloak and produced a rather large crystal orb. He cradled it in his hands as it glowed a pulsating silver light.. It hummed a low tone that bore into the bones of the onlookers. "Come close. Each of you must touch the orb as I say the words. The gate to the other world will open and then we will bring back one of the old ones with us."

Mickel watched the other figures stretch towards the orb. Human hands, claws, tentacles, and a translucent formless appendage all gripped the orb.With his hand completing the circle, the intensity of the illumination grew until a glowing cool silver light filled the whole space of the orb, and sliced through the arch's darkness.

Magnus lifted the orb aloft while saying "The vessel is ready. Make haste. We must cross the boundary between our world and the next."

He turned to the arch, and muttered "Oscail Doras na Rósaí."

Swirling golden light spiraled up the arch's supporting columns. Rainbow colored vines sprouted leaves that grew and died, re-sprouting again to turn to dust. It was a living and dying energy. The beams continued to twist around the arch until they collided in the middle. A large golden rosebud formed from the mingling of the light, its petals pulled away as it bloomed, a rainbow-flowing liquid seeping down over the opening in the middle. Where it struck the ground it flowed back to the bases of the columns, twisted back up the vines, and redistributed from the rose. It was a perpetual flow of rainbow fluid and colors.

Magnus handed the orb to the closest figure to his right. "Agatha, guard this with your life."

Agatha, who looked like something crossed between an insect and a human, both beautiful and horrifying, nodded their head, and pulled the orb towards their chest.

Magnus turned back to the arch, gripping it tightly he said, "Taispeáin Dom an Cosán"

The waterfall of iridescent energy parted down the middle, leaving behind a dark void. The forest, which was visible beyond the veil of energy, was lost in the darkness. Figures approached, leaning in close as if to catch a glimpse of something within those shadows.

Magnus joined them, carefully stepping closer to the arches. Magnus stepped in through the dark slowly at first. His posture changed and he spun around. "Come! Join me!"

Mickel was not the first of the remaining fourteen through, but even as he took his first step, he wondered if the smooth dark glass would hold him. It did, however, as it did for the others, and soon enough he was traipsing along in the dark, his old world left behind.

~Part Two~

Mickel followed as the fourteen descended deeper into the void. His fellow acolytes stayed close together, near the silver orb, as Magnus hummed and seemed to bounce along ahead. As the path widened, Mickel found himself shoulder to shoulder with another, and he held back every fiber of his being to push in closer as the edge of the void threatened to take him. Loud screeches, growls and moans reverberated through the void's inky blackness.

The serpentine path continued under Mickel's feet, going from the smooth feeling of glass to the crunch of gravel. "We are almost there," Magnus called, his pace quickening.

Mickel pressed the others forward in an attempt to keep pace with Magnus.

A dull light glowed ahead as they neared the end of the path, and soon enough they came across a crystalline wall of green, glowing just enough to fend off the void. Through a small archway in the wall, they found a throne of similar material, glowing even brighter as lichen spread and twisted up the legs and back. They gathered in a semicircle with Magnus at the forefront.

A silence settled on the group. Growls and screeches from the void, echoed off the wall. The fifteen Unseen Council members stepped closer to the silver orb to escape the wisps of the shadows surrounding them.

The beat of hoofs echoed in the chamber, silencing all other noises. Eyes, stalks, long ears, and trails of smoke turned left and right within hooded cloaks as the group huddled together, attempting to zero in on the sound.

Through a glass arch on the left, sharp horns, adorned with draping moss and twisting metals pushed through from the dark, followed by a deer with not two, but three eyes that glowed a brilliant white. As it approached the throne, the beast rose to a staggering height and walked on its hind legs.

Mickel's heart raced as the creature stared at the others, pausing at each one, until it reached him. A surge of energy tingled through his body as the horned being's eyes pierced into his mind. Mickel's life flashed before his eyes, as if the being was dredging up the memories, pausing at points of pain in his life. When the eyes pulled away from him, Mickel let out a gasped breath, clutching the sides of his head. The strange creature left his mind floating in a sea of jumbled thoughts.

Time flashed before his eyes, while sounds whistled past his ears. The agony brought him to his knees. Mickel looked at the others surrounding him and noticed the ones that had experienced the staring contest assumed a similar position.

Mickel noted that the last one still standing was Magnus the moment he and the deer's eyes met. Instead of falling to his knees, Magnus stood firm, and the energy emanating from the two tore through the air and racked Mickel's mind. Flashes of light formed into images in his mind. Forests rose and fell. Men built villages, towns, cities, and metros. There were wars fought, some won and others lost. Death, birth, love, and loss all played out in his mind's eye.

He glanced back to Magnus and saw the sweat dripping down his face, while eyes were still locked with the beast.

Mickel wondered how the man could stand it. It had only been mere seconds for Mickel but felt like he had passed through years. How was Magnus continuing to stare down this creature? No, not creature. This ancient being was no mere creature with eyes that could peer so deep into reality. The only thing that could do that was a god, and the only god who looked as this being did was Cernunnos. This was the God *Cernunnos, God of the Wilds and Forrest*. The thought raced through his head like a bolt of lightning, causing more pain in its wake. He looked towards their fearless leader and the God. They had ended their battle of wits. Magnus braced against his knees, looking ready to puke. The God on the other hand sat calmly in its throne, legs crossed. Again the eyes swirled between the occupants.

Mickel was less afraid when the eyes fell on him again, but the power still tingled his spine.

"WELCOME TRAVELERS." A booming voice, deep and sonorous like that befitting a god, echoed. "WHY HAVE YOU COME?"

Mickel snatched his hands over his ears again, little good it did as the voice ripped through his mind. The others gathered before *Cernunnos* clasped the sides of their heads in similar agony.

"Mickel Magaid, Mage. Your blood is pure from the old lands. You shall be the bearer."

~Part Three~

Mickel opened and closed his fists, looking around at the others. They didn't hear it. They didn't know *Cernunnos* had named him the bearer. Why? Why him? What was he supposed to—

Magus stepped forward and genuflected before the great God. "Great Horned One, we assembled before you to offer our services. The world you once knew and wondered through has changed in a way that we cannot fathom. People have forgotten the old ways. They worship at the feet of a new God. They claim to understand him and speak on his behalf, yet do terrible things in his name. We seek to bring back some of our power, to revolutionize the world, to bring back and worship in the old ways. The Pagan ways. Your ways, great Cernunnos." He lowered his head in sublimation.

"THE OLD GODS ARE EITHER FORGOTTEN OR LONG SLEEPING IN THEIR OLD HALLS. WHY SHOULD I HELP YOU?"

"You are one of the oldest and most powerful. The God of the Wilds and the wilds itself cannot die. You could bring back the old ways and your fellow Gods. You would change the world for the better. Wouldn't that be worth a few drops of your blood?"

Mickel watched the old God, wondering about what it had said in his mind. If he was to be the bearer, then surely Cernunnos had already made up their mind, or was that only a prediction? He thought about speaking but didn't know what to say. He tried to keep his thoughts on the conversation but felt that his energy was slowly slipping away.

Cernunnos stared at the man for a moment more. With a flick of their wrists, the hooves popped off their arms, clattering to the floor. In their place, hands emerged. Mickel almost laughed audibly, at the strange sight. Agatha stepped forward holding the crystal ball. The

God leaned from their great throne, till the massive face was mere inches from Agatha.

The hand stretched towards the vessel, and once it made contact, a drop of green blood smeared across the surface of the orb. The God lifted their finger away and the blood seeped through the surface, filling the crystal. Its green color morphed to a bright golden hue.

The God returned to their upright position, sucking on the finger to stop the flow of blood. Mickel couldn't keep his eyes off of the glowing globe, cradled in Agatha's arms. He felt a pull into the globe. It sang to him in a sweet voice.

"Carry us back and reap the reward." Mickel heard in his mind.

He reached out for the globe, and when his hands touched, heat emanated and raced up his arms. It swirled around his heart and tripped up to his brain. Golden light glowed from his eyes and shot upwards. The light filled the cavern reflecting off the crystal throne. It highlighted the face of the old God, accentuating the curves of the horns and the sharpness of their cheeks. The shadows contrasted to make the old one more terrifying.

Mickel's hand snapped from the surface of the golden orb as Magnus grabbed him. The golden light splintered away plunging the group back in the wash of green and dark.

~Part Four~

"What do you think you were doing?" Magnus hissed.

Mickel felt a strange euphoria flowing through his veins. He was warm and happy and wanted to hug everyone around him. "It called to me. Cernunnos told me that I was to carry the orb back to the world."

The older man turned towards the old one. "Lord Cernunnos, is it true that you asked him to carry the orb back to our world?"

The dear God titled his head, "Yes, this one will be the bearer. You dare question my commands?" This time the words actually came from the beast's mouth.

"No of course not Lord. I just thought the honor would be mine."

Cernunnos righted its massive head, smirking. "No, my dear child. You are to remain here as part of me."

With that, the old one grabbed the man about the waist and dragged him upwards. The creature unhinged its jaws, showing a mouth full of razor-sharp teeth.

"No! Wait! My Lord, please!" Magnus shouted, clawing at the massive hand that wrapped around his waist.

Mickel looked towards the other compatriots, yet they were frozen staring straight ahead. Agatha still knelt holding the golden orb aloft in her hands. Mickel waved a hand in front of her face. She didn't even blink. Nothing had affected them.

Mickel's attention was again drawn to the horror happening above his head. The jaws of the monster had widened and it was holding Magnus above its mouth.

Magnus screamed in horror again, thrashing harder to become free but the old God lifted him above their head and lowered Magnus into their mouth, snapping it shut. The bones and sinew crunched as Cerunnos chewed, while blood seeped from the corners of their mouth, matting the brown fur of their body.

The man who had brought them all together and began the revolution was dead.

Mickel looked towards the others who had journeyed together as they came out of their trances. They looked around the space until Agatha spoke up. "Magnus? Where has he gone?"

The blank stares made Mickel wonder if their minds were even there anymore. He lifted the orb from the hands of Agatha. The intensity of the glow increased, filling the space with the magical light.

"Now leave this place. Return to your world and release me before dawn's first light, Mickel," Cernunnos said.

"Follow me!" Mickel called out. "I will lead you back. Everyone stay close to me. Hold on to each other and keep your eyes on the golden glowing orb. We will be back into the world shortly."

He started moving up the path they had descended. The glow played strange tricks on the shadows, casting them into odd shapes, haunting figures, and dangerous objects. Mickel could feel the others form close behind him. There was less talking than when they had made their way to the throne. He kept a fast pace wanting to get out of the darkness. Mickel tried to figure out how much time had passed, but without any technology, it was impossible to tell. The path became less gravel leading back to the solid crystal–like substance underfoot. He guessed they had to be getting close. Then the rainbow-dripped door hung open above them. Through it, the first hints of dawn were lightening the sky. Mickel picked up the pace leading the party to the human world again.

Soon the now party of fourteen creatures tumbled out of the Adams Hall arch and onto the small circular ring of stones. As the last person stepped from the doorway, the magic rose that was above the archway shed its petals and disappeared. The door occupying the arch shrunk away only leaving the small grove of forest and the path leading into it.

Fog hung in the air, shimmering in the pre-dawn light, bringing a chill to Mickel and he shivered. The cloak that had kept out the rain had vanished in the night's adventures. The gathered creatures, though cloaked, also shivered in the morning's fog.

"Come on, we need to get to the pyramid to harness the power of the sun and release The Horned God. The revolution is nigh."

~Part Five~

The group made the very short jaunt to the pyramid structure that served as a chapel for the university students. Its doors unlocked in the early hours as the proprietors were preparing for a service. The group who had traveled into the next realm coming back with the essence of a God would be making this a service that no one would forget.

They entered the building, and although still moving in shocked silence, the group was able to get five candles lit and placed around the center. Their flames flickered and waved in the presence of the golden orb, which Mickel placed in the center of the raised dais. Thirteen hands, tentacles, claws and incorporeal limbs joined together forming a larger circle, around the dais connecting the group and the place. The group chanted calling forth the powers, to bring back the way of old, the ways of power, and the old ones. Mickel approached the orb, and lifting it above his head, the orb burned in a powerful glow. It's light-filled every nook and cranny of the sloped sides structure. The glow seeped down his arms and through his chest. It pulsed at his heart and coursed through his eyes.

A beam of light shot up, towards the apex of the pyramid. Smaller strands of light twisted and turned around the center beam. They swirled to and fro enchanting those gathered in their delicate dance. Light poured down through the bottom of the object and filtered through the surrounding group, linking them together. Each creature filled with a golden hue, from the midsection outwards. All sets of eyes produced beams of light that added to the central beam, making it stronger. The flutter of the hearts beat as one unit, pounding in chests pushing the light further and further out.

The first creature to Mickel's right became only light and was sucked into the next creature to the right. Then that creature burst into two balls of light and flowed into their neighbor. Each of the thirteen creatures absorbed the lights of the ones before it and then became nothing but light themselves, adding to the number of orbs. The final creature became light and then all moved into Mickel's body. The floating orbs of light pulsed inside of his now glowing body, pushing up his arms and out of his hands. They flowed up into the dancing streams becoming brighter and moving along an unheard rhythm.

Outside, a sudden shift in atmospheric pressure filled the sky with dark clouds. Lightning flashed through the sky and thunder crashed in the clouds. A bolt flared through the roof cascading down towards the orb smacking into it with a furry. The crystal orb that held the ancient blood of an un-worshiped God cracked, splitting in perfect half spears. The liquid that it contained swam up into the light turning the light to bright gold and crimson.

Mickel was sucked up into the swirl of power. Red and gold swirled throughout his body. The glowing light beat feverishly inside the chapel and him. Lightning swooped down and struck him.

The light rave blinked out of existence, coalescing into his body, which dropped towards the floor.

~Part Six~

Cernunnos opened the eyes of its new body. The body that would carry out the coming age of retribution and revolution. Having human flesh, limbs and extremities amused the old God. They flexed fingers, and toes and waved arms and legs. Tensed and popped joints. It had been a long time since the God had felt like that. The desire to run in the wilds swelled up in the old being, they pushed towards the living world.

Grass damp with dew and thick fog crunched under the new feet, while colors flashed by its head. The birds' sharp cries priced the gods' ears, and the rain tingled their nose. Cernunnos was free from the prison. Free from the forgotten and un-worshiped. They would raise the places of new worship.

The creature turned back towards where it was released. With a wave of its hand, large green vines erupted from the ground and pierced the building's walls. They pulled and pulled until the walls and roof collapsed. Another cock of its head brought a large tree, of twisting bark and limbs, shooting towards the heavens. The tree crashed through the remainder of the roof and moved skywards.

The old creature smiled at its work.

One down, many more to go.

ABOUT PATRICK J. MURPHY III

Patrick J. Murphy III (he/him) writes Paranormal Fantasy, Neo-Noir, YA Romance, and Poetry. He was born in Chicago and grew up in Columbus Ohio, where he attended Ohio State University for theater and film studies. Patrick is a member of Rockford Area Writers.

He has previously been published in *Writers on the Fox: A Short Collection of the Musings, Memoirs and Mysteries of a Magical Group: The Writers on the Fox, Tell Me About It 3: LGBTQ Secrets, Confessions, and Life Stories and Tales of Wonder and Dread: A Collection of Science Fiction and Horror Tales* anthologies. He also self-published *Thunder and Lightning* and *Doppelganger* from the *Writers on the Fox Anthology* in 2020.

Patrick currently lives in Rockford, Illinois where he does volunteer board work for The LIAM Foundation, a non-profit organization focusing on the needs of the LGBTQIA+ community. As a member of the LGBTQIA+ community, he feels that it is important to "share our stories, teachings, and history". When not writing, Patrick enjoys reading, watching Netflix, and cooking.

You can find out more about Patrick on his website PMurphyAuthor.com, or by following him on social media.

THE RITUAL

BY CATRINA BRIGHTON

C laire winced, pulling off her glasses and placing them on top of her notebook. She leaned back in her stiff plastic chair and stared up at the ceiling. The shrill laughter continued from two aisles over, in what Claire guessed was the comedy section.

She checked her phone. The laughter had only been happening for about ten minutes, but it felt like it had been hours. The Rockford Public Library was usually much quieter and less packed than her college campus library. The library always had a consistent crowd, but they usually were respectfully quiet. Today, it was like it had become the most popular summer hangout spot for bored teens. It was almost as loud as it was at home. She looked over at the private study rooms. All still occupied. She spied the front desk.

The library intern, who looked like a teen herself, glared towards the noise. The front desk she worked at was covered with clutter. Stacks of books and loose papers formed a barrier between her and the public. The intern locked eyes with Claire for a brief second before turning away sheepishly and burying herself back in her laptop.

Claire put her glasses back on and returned to her phone, pulling up the calendar. She had work the next three days, but Wednesday was completely open after class. She'd come back and get a private study room. Her photography exam was at the end of the month, leaving her two weeks to study. She reminisced back to when she fell in love with photography, back in high school. Going to college to do photography as a business had sucked most of the joy out of it. Especially this recent semester.

Her professor, Mrs. Welch, had no energy, fun, or even basic enthusiasm in her lectures. Her monotone voice was low and heavy. It made class tedious, and a few hours stretched into what felt like years. Students would regularly nod off or play around on their laptops, like Claire did. Now an exam loomed over Claire's head, and she was panicking.

Claire opened her backpack and began packing up. The teens could have the library today. She jumped at another burst of laughter, dropping her notebooks to the floor, her printed exam results spilling everywhere. In large, bold, red lettering "Failed" written across the top. Claire shoved the exam in the bottom of her backpack forcing her notebooks on top.

"What do you think of this take?" A hushed voice asked. It was followed by music that was quickly turned down. Claire stood, pushing her auburn curls away from her ears. She walked an aisle down and listened. Through the books she saw the loud ones. They weren't teens. She had seen them at her college before. Two guys and a girl in a sparkly red mini dress huddled over a phone.

Claire recognized the girl as her classmate, Tiffany Strand. Tiffany came from money and her parents paid her tuition so it didn't matter if she failed her exams. She had a built-in safety net.

"It's great! I think we finally got it right!" Tiffany replied in a low voice. She giggled, pressing the phone screen.

Claire could just make out a tiny version of Tiffany doing an elaborate dance on screen. She wore an oversized, obnoxiously bright unicorn onesie. The top of her hoodie, a giant unicorn head, flopped around vigorously as she danced. Her long blonde wavy hair hit her in the face, getting tangled up in the unicorn's horn. She jumped up and when she landed wore the outfit Tiffany was currently wearing. She got close to the camera and mouthed the lyrics to the song. She winked and blew the camera a kiss.

Claire walked out of the aisle and sighed. All that noise for some dumb video? It must be nice to not worry about any real problems. She returned to her cramped table and took out her notebook again. It sounded like the noisy idiots were leaving. She could finally study in peace.

Claire saw the group walk into the hallway. She rolled her eyes.

"Hey wait, I gotta do the ritual. Do you have a pen?" Tiffany asked the taller of the two guys. He quickly handed her a pen.

Claire's dark brown eyes darted up at the group. There was a ritual? She watched as the group walked past her table headed down the aisle directly in front of it. They gathered at the end of that aisle facing a section on the right.

Tiffany scanned rows of books on the shelf, an outstretched finger pointing at each title. She grabbed a well worn blue book off the shelf and placed it on the table at the end of the aisle. She clicked the pen, opened the cover, and leaned over to write something. Her hair cascaded over her shoulder blocking the view.

"That's a good one," the taller of the two guys said with a little nod. He leaned in with his phone and snapped a picture.

Tiffany giggled and handed the pen back to the guy. She closed the book, returning it to the shelf. They talked in hushed tones as she and the guys walked out of the aisle heading towards the library exit.

Did those idiots really write in a book? Who does that? As soon as they were out the door, Claire rushed down the aisle. She found the book quickly and burst it open. There was a pink post-it note on the first page. In neat handwriting, it read "Hey there, sunshine! Remember, every cloud has a silver lining, and your brightest days are just around the corner. Keep that smile shining and let your positivity light up the world. You've got this!" At the bottom there was a crudely drawn sun with a smiling face and a rainbow with clouds.

Claire stifled a laugh. "Wow, that's so cheesy. Straight cringe." She removed the note, crumpling it up in her fist. It's easy to be positive when your life is perfect.

Claire's phone buzzed as she returned to her table, a text message from her boss asking if she'd pick up a shift. Making sandwiches sounded completely unappealing at the moment. Her brows furrowed as she considered her options. Studying was important, but so was paying for her college classes. Plus, it would keep her out of the house for a few extra hours. Claire hastily packed up her stuff and headed out before she could talk herself out of it.

Once Wednesday's class ended Claire went back to the library. She was in luck, there were two private study rooms available. She chose the one further away from the cramped public tables she sat at before. The room was a plain beige color, with no art or decorations. It had a large table, a padded chair, and outlets to charge your devices. The large wooden door kept the noise out and provided a small window to see out of. Next to the door, there was a larger glass window facing out towards the rest of the library, perfect for people watching.

Claire pulled up her phone's calendar app. Noting the dates, she scheduled a library study session, four days a week, for the next two weeks. It would be challenging for sure. Between Mrs. Welch's mind-numbing class lectures, and being low staffed at the sandwich shop, the next two weeks would be long and draining. But the hope of passing the exam was all that mattered to Claire.

Claire settled in, pulling out her notebooks and laptop. At the bottom of her bag she spotted her failed exam and- a flash of pink? She smoothed out the wad of pink paper. It was Tiffany's dumb note. The sunshine doodle at the bottom had smudged, making one of the sun's eyes much larger than the other. The note stuck to the exam, wrinkled in the same way the exam was, as if they belonged together. Although the note was still cheesy, Claire couldn't help but smile at it, like the written version of some sitcom tv coach giving you a pep talk after you lost the big game. A warm and fuzzy feeling took hold in her chest.

Claire peered out into the library towards the section she found the book. Was there another note inside? She pushed the thought aside. She had to study. She opened her notebook, reviewing last week's class notes.

The pink post-it note caught her eye again. Had Tiffany and her dumb friends been back here?

Claire shook her head as if to shake the thought away, her curls gently hitting the sides of her pale face. "Study, you idiot," she patted her cheeks. "Focus! You can't afford to fail this class." She slid the exam under her laptop.

After a while Claire's notes started to blur together. She blinked hard, stretching her arms over her head. Her sweater sleeves slid down, revealing several small faded scars on her forearms. She adjusted her sleeves and stood, noting the time she shut the laptop lid. She'd been at it for an hour. A tiny break couldn't hurt. Perhaps even a break outside of this room, to get some fresh air? Maybe even a casual stroll down a certain aisle, just to stretch of course.

Claire shut the door behind her and headed towards the aisle. She got to the shelf, but what was the name of the book? She scanned the titles, but nothing seemed familiar. She only remembered that it was blue, with a worn spine. A few pulls later, she found it. "Healing

Hearts, Restoring Minds: Understanding and Overcoming the Struggles of Depression".

A book on depression? Tiffany was pretty, popular, and rich! What did Tiffany have to be depressed about? Did she even read this book?

Claire opened the cover. No note. She put the book back on the shelf with a little more force than needed.

Back in her private room Claire sat down to resume her studies but her mind was racing. "Is she serious right now? If anyone should be depressed, it's me! I have a shitty job, I'm constantly broke. I have no friends. My parents are divorcing. The only thing keeping my grades up is my attendance. If I fail this test, I'll fail the whole class, and I can't afford to take this class again," she fumed. "Tiffany didn't even come to class today!"

Something clicked in her brain. Tiffany didn't come to class today. Was it because of depression? Just as quickly as it appeared, the thought was beat down. Tiffany was probably just filming another stupid video.

Soon it was Saturday afternoon, the last day of her four day study session this week. This time Claire was smarter, she kept booking her private study room in advance. She set up quickly and jumped right into her notes. Though Mrs. Welch's lectures were still boring and dry, Claire managed to write down much more in her classes. Now it was just a matter of reviewing it all.

Her familiar failed exam, with its pink badge of encouragement, sat next to her stack of notebooks. Claire reread the post-it note, a tiny grin appeared on her face. It had been ages since she had had any encouragement from anyone. Her parents only seemed to speak in yells, as did her boss when she was at the sandwich shop. Even if it was fake encouragement from a stranger, it still felt nice. It still gave that warm and fuzzy feeling. A quick check down the aisle couldn't hurt, right?

"Hey there, sunshine! Remember, even the darkest clouds can't hide your sparkle. So chin up, smile on, and let your radiance light up the world. Your happiness is a gift worth sharing – let's turn those frowns into crowns!" The bottom of the pink post-it note had the same sun as before, paired with a poorly drawn pointy crown. This new post-it note was just as corny as the last. Claire let out a soft laugh as she shook her head. However, there was a warm feeling rising in her chest.

Claire slid the book back on the shelf, but carried the note back to her private room. It joined the other pink post-it note. Both notes were cheesy and over the top, but also strangely comforting. Claire found herself glancing over them often as she studied. Her little morale boosters.

On Monday and Tuesday Claire checked the aisle after her studies. No new note. The last two Wednesdays had notes though, so on Wednesday Claire checked the aisle first. No new note. Claire slouched, walking slowly to her private room. She leaned back in her chair, closing her eyes. After a moment passed, an idea came to her.

She taped the two post-it notes to the inside of her laptop. She threw her old exam in the trash bin. It was a fresh start, a cleaned slate. Though her four day study sessions were still stale, Claire found it easier each day. And it was still better than going home and listening to her parents fight all night.

Claire packed it up and checked the aisle once more, just in case. Still nothing. She ran her fingers over the title. Maybe the whole book was like a long form of Tiffany's note?

Claire opened the book and skimmed through the pages. It was surprisingly technical. Little illustrations and diagrams were sprinkled throughout. A large picture of a brain greeted her, little blurbs noting all its different sections. The chapters were short, but each seemed packed with information. Claire felt the same warm feeling bubbling in her chest. She closed the book and took it over to the self check out area.

Thursday, after Mrs. Welch's class, Claire rushed over to the library. Once she was in her study room she'd get started right away. She headed over to her private study room, but someone was inside. A guy with large headphones, head bobbing along, with a large laptop In front of him.

Claire pulled out her phone. She'd forgotten to book her room for today. All the remaining rooms were taken. She sighed. At least her cramped public table was available.

She glanced up at the wall clock. One-thirty. If she hurried, she could get her study session done early and read more of her book before her shift tonight. Claire set up her laptop in front of her, notebooks to the side, and her library book on top of them. She pulled her hair back out of her face and got to work.

Tiffany walked by Claire's table, phone in hand, and a photography book tucked in under her arm. She was swiping vigorously on the screen when she spotted Claire's book.

"Oh, I loved that book. It helped me a lot," Tiffany pointed at the book with a big smile.

When did she get here? Had she seen the post-it notes? Claire was startled out of her study trance. "Y-Yeah?" Claire stuttered, slamming her laptop lid closed. She faced Tiffany, elbow on the table to block the view of her device. "What was your favorite part?"

Tiffany shifted a little. "Hmmm... probably the stuff about chang-ing your mindset," she confirmed with a small head nod. "I used to be so negative. Always beating myself up. Then I worked on changing my negative core beliefs and quieting my inner critic."

It was hard to believe that Tiffany ever had a negative thought in her life, let alone beat herself up. But Claire was intrigued. "Negative core beliefs?"

"Yeah, the book will explain it better than I can. But, it's just stuff like... 'I'm stupid', 'No one loves me', 'I'm a failure' stuff like that." Tiffany let out a nervous giggle. "Once you learn to fight that stuff, you'll be a lot happier." She pushed some hair behind her ear, nodding her head once more.

Claire glanced at the book with a smirk. It was hard to believe that she could ever be as cheery as Tiffany seemed, but if she could be just a little more positive? It was worth a chance. "Well, thanks. I'll let you know how it goes."

Tiffany smiled. "If you ever need to talk or something, let me know."

Claire's brows furrowed. "Why are you being so nice to me? You never talk to me in class."

Tiffany's cheeks flushed. "To be fair, I don't talk to anyone in class. I'm too busy fighting to stay awake." She gestured to the book once more. "You're going through hell. I know what that's like, I went through it too. All I wanted was someone who would listen. Someone who could understand. But I was alone."

Tiffany put her photography book down on the table. She pulled out a chair and took a seat on the other side of Claire. "So after I read this book, I wanted to, you know... pay it forward somehow." She dug around in her purse for a moment before pulling out the bright pink post-it notes.

Claire put up a hand to pause her. "I know." Slowly, she opened up her laptop and spun it around to face Tiffany. Claire lowered her face towards the table, her face a bright crimson.

Claire waited a moment, just staring at the table waiting for Tiffany to say something. But nothing came. The awkward silence became too much. Just as Claire lifted her head to speak, she felt her laptop move.

Tiffany turned the laptop to face Claire.

Claire looked at it. There was a new post-it note next to the other two. "I'm your Going Through Hell Buddy now! Don't give up! Boring lectures can't stop us! We got this!" A tiny thumbs up and crying-laughing smiley face were drawn at the bottom.

Claire and Tiffany hung out for a little bit. They reviewed Claire's notes together and quizzed each other. They exchanged phone numbers before Tiffany left.

Claire walked up to the front desk once Tiffany was gone. "Hey, can I borrow a post-it note?" The intern handed her a pale yellow one.

"I know it sounds fake, but I believe in you. One day, you'll believe in you too." Claire pressed the note into the book. Simple, maybe even a little boring, but it was genuine. A warm smile creeped onto her face and she chuckled. "Oh god, I'm becoming a Tiffany!" She hadn't finished reading the book yet, but her note was waiting in place for the next reader.

On Exam Day morning, Claire was a little jittery. Racing thoughts started to flood in. Her chest was tight, hands clammy. She was determined to not let her anxiety get the best of her. Claire took a deep breath. She had studied daily for weeks now. She had practice quizzes with Tiffany over text. She would be applying for scholarships to help out after class today. She had done everything she could and it was out of her hands now. She got dressed and headed out. Claire arrived early to class, coffee in hand.

Tiffany greeted her with a little wave and a thumbs up. "We got this."

Claire nodded, giving a thumbs up of her own.

Claire sat at her desk. She inhaled deeply, held it for a moment, then released it. She opened her laptop, Tiffany's friendly notes greeting her. "You can do this!" She thought. And though she had no proof, this time she actually believed it. Claire loaded up her exam and got to work.

ABOUT CATRINA BRIGHTON

Catrina Brighton is relatively new to the writing world but comes with a background primarily in the arts. She has a passion for exploring themes related to human connections and mental health. Catrina believes that people are rich sources of stories, whether shared or observed. Her work is a fusion of these observations, making her writing truly captivating. Thank you for taking the time to read her work, and if you'd like to discover more about Catrina, please visit instagram.com/catrina.brighton.

WALKING TOWARDS FREEDOM: SOME NOTES FROM A JOGGER ON ROCKFORD'S NORTHSIDE

BY LUKE MCGOWAN-ARNOLD

Walking and exploring our natural and created environment is a lost art to some. Not to people in Rockford, though. One foot in front of the other. Clearing your mind. Observing the world. Watching the tired human geography. People sit idly at bus stations. They wait expectantly at crosswalks. They cut through yards. They smoke weed while traversing a park. All while walking somewhere. A destination in mind even if it isn't necessarily a physical one. Traveling even in a small way helps us to define ourselves through our surroundings. I wonder often about the nature of American society and how our walks can help us find that nature. But some questions are necessary first.

What is American society? How can we define it through walking around a place like Rockford, Illinois? How does simply walking around and taking in your surroundings help us to grasp the realities of this American society? America is a country that is full of contradictions, diversity, and an abundance of perspectives. As someone who comes from a legacy of enslaved Africans in Virginia and Irish working class immigrants in Pennsylvania, there is no doubt in my mind that America is utterly subsumed in the class struggle that is shaped and molded by race. As much as they tell us to believe that it exists as a land of opportunity, the material realities reveal themselves.

I believe that these contradictions are some of the strongest in my hometown of Rockford, Illinois. If you understand Rockford, you can understand American society in my view. It exists as a microcosm. Jogging around my neighborhood helps me understand Rockford. There are many narratives about the city improving that have been popularized in recent years; my jogs through the neighborhood seem to dispute these narratives. I started jogging again to get out of my head. It was the height of the pandemic. I didn't want to be inside all day. It just made sense. And I found some realities that while uncomfortable, I am glad to understand.

And well, running gets you to know the areas in which you live. It breaks apart any illusions that emerge from the colorful ad campaigns and shiny new hotels downtown. The murals can't cover up the poverty, violence, abandoned furniture factories, predatory payday loan places, and the general urban desolation. I take the position of a materialist that our material world defines our society, not constructed narratives that are pushed by the rich and powerful. We must explore and fully embrace the material world in order to understand what it will take to shape this.

I take a route from my home in the Rockford neighborhood of Edgewater up North Main to Loves Park and then back around on the bike path to my parent's home. I jog over sidewalks filled with overgrown grass and past abandoned storefronts where the Taco John's used to be. I have been walking these streets and riding along bike paths for most of the years of my small life. There is a comic store in Loves Park that I spent a lot of time in while in high school. I would play a Star Wars themed roleplaying game with my friends until the shop closed. We would walk down the strip in Loves Park for pizza, staring into forever.

I typically begin my runs at sunset with only an audiobook for accompaniment. Or maybe it's a new track from 23Sonny or Piff Mason, two young legends from the West Side. Or a throwback track from JudahTheLyricalRev. Rockford Files is a good one. If you know, you know. Shoutout to all my real Rockford hip hop heads. Regardless of what I'm listening to, my run takes me up North Main past Village Green where my mom wanted my brother to work and past where the old Blockbuster used to be. Back when I was in elementary school, I remember hearing a story about a kid who got hit by a car and died when crossing North Main. Despite this, it is one of the nicer roads on the West Side. Small bars, restaurants and gas stations line the sides. As I cross the railroad tracks, I see two Ford Explorers with their red and blue lights flashing. Just another day. My brother, when he was a teen, was stopped and harassed by the RPD with his friends (all young black men) while they were playing basketball. The police placed him and his childhood friends in their Ford Explorer or maybe it was a different car...that was years ago and police are always getting new toys. The RPD rode them around asking questions about drugs they had no idea about. Apparently, RPD are supposedly our friends now because they have community houses where they do art classes, but every year another name is added to the long list of Rockford residents they've killed.

There's a lot of abandoned storefronts as I jog along. There used to be a factory near the Rosecrance building. I remember after that white supremacist murdered Heather Heyer in Charlottesville, some-one had clambered up the building and done some graffiti that read "Death to Fascism" or something along those lines. It was covered up later. I'm pretty sure there are some anarchists or radical malcontents living somewhere on the Northside as I often find graffiti which reads "Fuck the Police" or with anarchy As throughout on my jogs, though it seems the anarchist(s) have been less busy recently. I don't count myself among them due to my own lack of political bravery but I share their critique of the American world in Rockford, Illinois.

In 2020, on May 30th, "out of town anarchists and agitators" were blamed for the riot. I was busy at home working on my senior college coursework that day but I remember the city leaders and supposed "black leaders" coming out the next day to decry the protests as somehow the work of people from outta town. And yet, when I decided to check the arrest records, everyone arrested was from Rockford. The videos I saw seemed to be mostly young black and brown youth yelling about how their lives mattered and how they wanted the RPD to stop killing them. Then the police beat and tear gassed those young people. Could it be that the poor in this city have their own reasons to hate the police?

In some ways, the politically combative nature of American society is evident throughout my run. The police are harassing people. The radical graffiti. I'll see cars with confederate flags or "don't tread on me" flags riding by. Everyone wants to fight. That's the history of American society. Class and racial conflict is inscribed into every mile. On this August evening as I run, things seem serene but it will only take another moment for things to explode again.

As someone who has spent much time on the East Coast, I often hear the idea that the Midwest is just a bunch of racist white people. Places like Rockford that voted for Trump in 2016 and 2020. People place our city into a box. Rockford is a different America from the skyscraper lined glass cities on the Coast, according to the journalists. A white racist America. But for me who takes walks, the perception that there are "different Americas" is one of the most ludicrous things in the world. All people in the United States are bonded together through our lived histories and environments. The land that the city of Rockford and all of the United States is built upon was stolen from indigenous people. They are not here anymore though, only the strip mall on North Main. But the conflict is not gone. It simply changes.

The North Towne mall is the happening spot if happening means a Mexican restaurant, a biker bar, a pawn shop where my brother buys ceremonial swords, a McDonalds, a few other stores I'm forgetting, and a bank. I do love the Swedish pancakes at the aptly named "Swedish Pancake House". Despite this, the desolation is palpable: shitty service jobs with minimum wage and shitty places to spend what little money you make from those jobs. We can't forget the liquor store. The emptiness of the parking lots in North Towne is a real look into the gnashing maw that is working class life under capitalism in a post-industrial area like Rockford. There is little social life here beyond alcohol. And it makes sense; the only people truly enjoying life in Rockford are the rich who pay for expensive drinks in some downtown restaurant that sacrifices the health and bodies of their workers on the sacred altar of "small local business".

Racialized capitalism forces us apart from one another. It makes a future impossible to believe or see or recognize. All of the initiatives in the city seem to be towards a future in Rockford that attracts capital. But that does not leave any hope for the oppressed and downtrodden. It does not seem like there is any hope of a better world for people in Rockford or the broader country. The dead end jobs don't offer it. The politicians don't offer it. The schools do not offer it. Despite this, the resurgence of conflict gives me hope. Conflict indicates that nihilism and apathy isn't the only trend in a place like Rockford. People are willing to fight. That's clear from every walk I take. Conflict is lingering under the surface. Hopefully, people are willing to fight for the right things.

During my run, I jog through Martin Park. Martin Park has a swamp. It is one of the more natural places in this area that is not completely paved over by concrete and such. I wonder often about who fights for the land. There seems to be a hopelessness about the environment and the reality of our ability to save it. The destruction of the Bell Bowl Prairie only serves to elucidate the helplessness of preserving nature. I think that the fundamental truth is that the future of the land is tied to the conflicts inherent to the American condition. I love the parks in Rockford. It is the Forest City. The parks were a part of socialist initiative in the local government back in the early 20th century. Shoutout to Mayor Bloom. There is futurity and hope in the land. In the greener spaces. Though, I am unsure what exactly this futurity is. It feels appropriate that the largest protest in Rockford's history on May 30th, 2020 began in the public park. People found themselves together in a park filled with trees, a common space, and imagined a better world without racism and police violence.

Our city has gotten increasingly less white over the last 20 years. More Black people from Chicago have moved here as rents in the city continue to rise and there have been more Latino folks living here than ever before. The North Side has become less white and more multi-racial over the past 20 years. My friend Keivion told me a story about how his family moved there to the North Side. As a youth, he was questioned by the police about what he was doing in that neighborhood. There's a black owned Muslim hair store on North Main now. I jog by it regularly. Oh, how times change!

To reflect the changing times, the local city government has hosted Juneteenth events and other such things to prove their commitment to diversity. Despite this, the violence of the police and poverty continue to persist. Just take a jog through the Northside. The new murals go up downtown with images of Black queer people adorning the walls and yet I still know too many black trans women who struggle to find housing. I cannot imagine the hardship considering the harsh winters we face in Rockford. Symbolism only goes so far when it comes to a material reality.

Rockford is a good example to understand the declining nature of American society and how that is tied to the inherent truths that built this country. In particular, this Midwestern city represents the zeitgeist of the United States: the anarchist graffiti on the pole as the truck with the confederate flag bumper sticker and the police roll past; the gentrification downtown which contrasts with the desolation that is the North, South and West Sides. Rockford is supposedly improving according to the city officials but in my walks, it is clear that the only thing that is improving is the willingness of people in our society to fight one another in order to either preserve or transform the current state of things.

I think the importance of growing up and living in Rockford is that I have no misconceptions about the violence and contradictions within American society. Anything and everything is on display. I think that post-industrial Midwestern cities such as Rockford, which lack the glitz and glam of the newly built up centers of capital in the metropolis and the realities of American conflict, are more clear in a particular sense.

I think that cities like Rockford, despite desolation and alienation, offer a certain sense of hope. The profound lack of meaningful capital despite the efforts of the few gentrifiers means that in the wastelands such as Rockford, new forms of life can begin to take hold and new forms of social organization will emerge. I do not romanticize these areas. Despite this, I think there are possibilities here. The models offered by groups like Cooperation Jackson in Mississippi or Horizontal Stateline create a solidarity economy that are intriguing starts. I have given up political prescriptions. But we have to build a city that isn't just for the powerful. To hold ourselves together. To be accountable to one another. Not landlords. Not city leaders. Not the bosses. Not the police. Not the jailers. Perhaps this begins with a jog and conversations about freedom.

The divisions between those who want freedom and the people that don't are more clear and less obscured here than in the big cities I've been in. I think that the proximity of people to one another matters in Rockford. This is different in big cities as the classes often exist in completely separate worlds. Obviously, there is no absolute way to describe this. However, I do think the smaller scale means it makes it harder for the oppressors to dial down the everyday social conflict that exists within American society. You must know what side your neighbor is on. I see confederate flags everyday in Rockford. To me, that's a good thing because it means I have no illusions about American racism.

And then my run comes to a close. I pass by the same things every run. Poverty, racism, conflict, nature, development, nihilism, hope, and most of all, uncertainty. One of the factories along North Main has been torn down. That was where the graffiti against fascism was. Now, there's simply an empty lot until a developer builds something new. A new office for an aspiring start-up or something else that will continue to leave Rockford's poor behind.

My jog at some point takes me across the river. The river represents something, I think. A part of the natural world that despite being poisoned, remains resilient. In this way, that's how I feel about the oppressed in Rockford. Despite everything, they remain resilient. Youth spray paint slogans against fascism on the walls of dead factories and houses. May 30th Alliance and other rabble rousers continue to hold vigil at city hall for all those slain by the State as they read Angela Davis out loud over Facebook Live. Queer and trans activists from the Liam Foundation protest the presence of the RPD at the yearly Pride celebration hosted by The Office. Feminists meet up to discuss new abortion facilities opening in the city. Community gardens run by Pan-Africanists or punks or neighbors simply trying to spend more time outside emerge in various empty lots across the city. The workers at the Starbucks on East State organize a union and stage a walkout. There are conversations about the problems in our city in Davis Park, that ugly Discovery Center walkway, the loud Mary's place parking lot, in a quiet corner of Katie's Cup, and countless other spaces. These things happen for a while then they stop and then they happen again. And life continues on.

American society by nature is combative, conflictual and violent. There is no way to avoid this. It has always been this way and it always will be until it is entirely remade. As human beings we have to understand our own realities through engaging in constant material analysis of the world. The city leaders seek to fit the world into boxes (such as the hideous new developments) so we are unable to push forwards to a life that is worth living. Activists, organizers, artists, writers, anyone interested in social change must seek to break the boxes through grounding ourselves in what is real and material. We can do this by jogging around our neighborhoods.

Every segment of American society will take part in the coming conflict. The idea that some areas are too far gone or cannot be transformed socially is ridiculous and foolish. People with goals of progress, political revolution, social change or whatever you want to call it have to understand that to change American society, we have to engage with every geographic context in which the American people exist. I want a world defined by freedom for the many, not for the few. There are those who seek to oppose this. We must oppose them whether they are racist police, developers seeking to raise the rents, white supremacists, religious zealots who seek to oppose a woman's right to choose, and so on.

I will continue to run, walk, pace, or meander around my neighborhood wherever I may live. I'd encourage you to do the same if you are physically able. If not, take a drive. Maybe invite a friend, a lover, or a neighbor. Talk to them about the world you want to see in your city. Imagine what could be possible. What changes must happen and not simply changes that are aesthetic in their composition. Changes for everyone who isn't wealthy, who isn't white, who isn't straight or cis. A city for all of us, not just the few. I've taken plenty of walks and runs and strolls with friends in Rockford, I plan to take more. If we can grasp reality, we can grasp social change.

ABOUT LUKE MCGOWAN-ARNOLD

Luke Mcgowan-Arnold is a African-American writer from Rockford, Illinois. Being an African-American writer means he draws from African-American literary and cultural traditions in his work while trying to address themes of racism in the United States. Luke grew up on the West Side of Rockford.

He graduated from Auburn High School via the CAPA Program. Luke took Renaissance classes tootoo, but they didn't give him the medal because AP Stats seemed boring so he didn't take it and instead hung out in the library. You apparently need to take lots of math to be considered a Renaissance scholar. It feels important to include that because this is a bio for a Rockford based publication. He's still mad about not getting the medal even though he graduated a long time ago.

Luke wrote and released a concept album called "Rustbelt Radio" about Rockford, Illinois in 2021 with some of his friends under the nom de guerre "Huey, the Cosmonaut". He continues to make and release music under this name.

He lives in Philadelphia when he's not in Rockford, Los Angeles or Mexico City. And yes, he considers all of those cities to be within the same purview of splendor.

When he isn't writing or making music, he enjoys eating, riding on Amtrak, Muay Thai (kick-boxing from Thailand where you use your knees and elbows) and sweating profusely. You can follow him on Instagram for memes, music and more @hueythecosmonaut.

BEFORE YOU GO

T hank you so much for reading, and I hope you enjoyed this collection of poetry, essays, and short stories from local Rockford writers.

Before you go, here's the deal. We're independent writers, and reviews are the best way to help spread the word and reach new readers. If you could spare a few seconds, please consider leaving an honest review on the platform you purchased this book from (if they have one) or in places like Goodreads, Storygraph, or other pages. Your support helps so much and is truly appreciated.

Sincerely,

Rockford Area Writers

ACKNOWLEDGEMENTS

The journey of assembling this anthology has brought me to some remarkable talents and incredibly supportive souls. First and foremost are the amazing writers who contributed their unique voices and stories. Your willingness to edit and refine your work has not only enhanced the quality of this anthology, but also enriched my experience as its curator. I extend my heartfelt thanks to each one of you for your dedication and artistry.

A special note of goes to Jenna Goldsmith, Rockford's Poet Laureate. Jenna, your expertise and keen editorial eye have helped to elevate the submissions to their brightest potential. Your guidance and skill have left an indelible mark on every page, and for this, I am deeply appreciative.

To Fatherless Print Posse, thank you so much for this stunning cover art! What you created encapsulates the spirit and essence of our anthology. Your vision has given this book an identity for both the contributors and the readers to resonate with.

This anthology is not just a collection of writings; it's a symbol of collaboration, creativity, and community. To everyone who played a part in bringing this project to life, your contributions have been invaluable. Thank you for being part of this wild journey.

JP Rindfleisch IX

LEARN MORE ABOUT ROCKFORD AREA WRITERS

If the stories in this anthology captivated you and you'd like more from these talented writers and other local authors, then check out https://rockfordareawriters.com/. Rockford Area Writers (RAW) is a community platform for writers in the Rockford, Illinois area, designed to foster growth and collaboration among writers, publishers, and craftspeople.

Founded in late 2022, RAW partners with local businesses like the indie bookstore, Maze Books, to promote events and uplift local writing. The group includes writers of all kinds, from authors to poets, and comic book artists.

Are you a local writer interested in joining this community? RAW welcomes writers of all backgrounds and experience levels. Membership is free, and joining is as simple as reaching out via email. For more details and to become a part of this nurturing and inspiring group, please visit https://rockfordareawriters.com/.